# FAR FROM HOME

## A COLLECTION OF THREE
## M/M SCIENCE FICTION NOVELLAS

# Madeleine Urban

Published by
Dreamspinner Press
4760 Preston Road
Suite 244-149
Frisco, TX 75034
http://www.dreamspinnerpress.com/

This is a work of fiction. Names, characters, places and incidents either are the product of the authors' imagination or are used fictitiously, and any resemblance to actual persons, living or dead, business establishments, events or locales is entirely coincidental.

Cover Art by Dan Skinner/Cerberus Inc.   cerberusinc@hotmail.com
Cover Design by Mara McKennen

ISBN: 978-0-9815084-0-5

Printed in the United States of America
First Edition
January, 2008

eBook edition available
eBook ISBN: 978-0-9815084-1-2

To my parents, especially my mom, who
introduced me to science fiction and fantasy when
I was young enough to make it a lifelong passion.

# Table of Contents

# Acknowledgments

A startling number of my ideas come from music. Music moves me and inspires ideas unlike anything I can come up with on my own. Entire worlds spring to mind, and then I just have to figure out how to translate the lush images in my head into text. It's happened often enough that my friends now go looking for songs they think will do the trick – and sometimes they're even successful. Between that and watching the world go on around me, my imagination goes wild, and I end up crafting stories that later I can't believe I wrote.

A few people helped make these three stories coalesce from the ether.

I wrote the first version of Enhanced after talking with a friend, Jan, about how we liked to cast story characters in our head so we knew what they looked like (and could enjoy them more!) The heart of this story was inspired by the song "Here With Me" by Dido.

I had the idea for Close Encounter after reading a science article about using genetic enhancement to beat disease. I wrote what was practically the finished product you see here in one sitting, as encouraged by my friend Jenny over IM. I would write a section, she'd read it and ask, "Is there more?" and I'd say "Yes." So she said, "Then keep going!" Five hours later the story was done.

Following the Sun has been extensively revised from its first version, but I love it even more as it is now. I wanted to write something for my beloved best friend Willow, and she loves romance; I wanted to include my passion, science fiction and fantasy. The bare bones idea for the plot was inspired by the song "Following the Sun" by Enigma.

I hope you enjoy reading these stories as much as I enjoyed writing them.


Lots of love,

Madeleine

THE two men ran like the hounds of hell were snapping at their heels, scrambling down the blank, unmarked passageway. One limped heavily, his dark pants even darker with blood. The bright red splashed on his white lab coat weighted it down so it didn't flap as he moved. When he stumbled and fell to one knee, the other stopped to go back a few steps and help him up before they started running again, panting hard. They collided as they ran around a corner, skidding frantically as they made for the end of the hall, the uninjured man reaching the door and punching at the keypad while the other caught up, gasping for breath. The pad beeped in the negative, flashing a red light, and the injured man pushed the other to the side with a huff and hit a series of keys — then the board flashed green just as they heard heavy footsteps echoing in the bare metal hallway.

"C'mon c'mon c'mon Ryne," Cary said shakily as he slung an arm around his friend's waist and helped him through the doorway. Once he could reach, Cary smacked his fist against the control pad. They turned to see what was bearing down on them, and Ryne let out a scared rush of air as the door slammed down just in time — so close that what was outside rammed into the metal.

"We are in deep shit," Ryne said as the sound of something beating on the door echoed around them. He sagged against Cary, whose metal-rimmed glasses were askew.

"You think?" Cary snapped back sarcastically, helping the redhead to a nearby stool.

"I told you we should have stayed out of it," Ryne muttered, favoring his leg and gritting his teeth as he sat and shifted it.

"*You're* the one who asked *me* to get involved!" Cary crouched down next to him, flipping his ponytail over his shoulder as he peeled back the bloody material. "This doesn't look good," he said, prodding at the deep slash, making Ryne hiss and jerk away.

"Quit poking it and find something to wrap it up with!"

Cary got up and rifled a nearby medical cabinet for a First Aid kit, sliding some other items into his lab coat pockets while he was at it. He came back and wrapped up Ryne's leg. "You want something for the pain?" he asked clinically.

"If there's a local, that would be best. No way I'm going to be able to stay off it," Ryne answered, leaning a little against the table behind him.

They both glanced at the door as the pounding suddenly stopped. "That doesn't reassure me," Cary muttered.

"Gimme that syringe. We've got to get moving. The deep freeze is the next room over," Ryne said. "We need the stim shots and adrenaline."

"I'll get them," Cary said, handing Ryne the needle and watching him inject the agent into the skin near the wound and numbing it.

Ryne slowly relaxed. "Shit, this is gonna be bad," he said lowly, looking at his leg. "Bastard got me real good."

"Yeah, well, you're the one who said humanity had to know," Cary said. "I was just as happy going along ignorant."

Ryne reached out and yanked on Cary's long white-blond tail of hair. "You're still ignorant," he razzed tiredly.

"Bastard. Quit being lazy and get your ass up," Cary said, though a slight smile curled his lips and he extended a hand to help.

They used more codes to access the next room – one that look eerily like a stainless steel morgue. Cary stopped and looked around. By the look on his face, he was really uncomfortable. "It smells weird in here."

"Stale." Ryne glanced at him as he hobbled to the control table in the center of the room. "Don't worry. They're not going to wake up and grab you," he said with a grin. "Yet."

Cary flipped him the finger as he walked over to peer inside the windows of some of the compartments. "Who are these guys again and why can we trust them?"

"I don't know if we can trust them. But they've got to be better than the alternative, right?" Ryne said. Cary shot him a glare and Ryne rolled his eyes. "These are Spec 4 V1s, originally totally human, then enhanced, back when the adjustments were still experimental and not available to the general public. Meaning they were like you and me once, not grown in a petri dish and taught by computers," Ryne said.

Cary shivered and crossed his arms. "How do you deal with this shit? Petri dishes and experimental gene splicing."

"Looking at the science of it," Ryne said distractedly as he accessed the computer. "I'd find all those code strings you're so in love with mind-numbing."

"Yeah, well, as least computers don't puke on you," Cary muttered as he walked along the wall. "Why are some of the doors popped?"

Ryne glanced up sharply. "Popped?"

Cary nodded. "Yeah, the seals are broken."

"Don't open those. The cryo failed. Whoever was in there..."

"Is dead?" Cary asked, voice rising as the color drained out of his face. He backed away from the wall slowly and walked to look over Ryne's shoulder at lists of names and statistics scrolling on the screen. "What are you looking for?"

"Eight of the ten bays are dead. The other two look to be good. The computer says no one's been in here for more than thirty years," Ryne said.

"Are they going to be able to help us?"

"They're military. We've got to fight fire with fire – even if we are pitting Version 1s against Version 3s," Ryne said.

"Is that like comparing Windows 77 to Windows 79?" Cary asked as Ryne keyed the wake-up sequences.

"Yeah, sorta. Only our Windows 77s had human brains to start with, not computer chips like the 79s," Ryne said, keying up profiles that started flashing on the screen. "This is the first one."

They both studied the lines of description on the monitor. "What is all this? Hyper-reflex, hyperforce... I understand the specialty: martial combat and the handle: 'Nighthawk'," Cary said, frowning.

"All the V1s were parts of crack military teams. They functioned as a unit and used code names, not so different from the Marines fifty years ago, before the V3s replaced the military," Ryne said. "The rest of it's probably a job description of some sort."

"Tell me again how you know all this stuff?" Cary asked plaintively.

Ryne glanced at him as his fair skin flushed. "I, uh, broke into the database once I started suspecting what was going on."

Cary grinned. "And you say you're not a computer nerd."

Ryne rolled his eyes and pointed off to the side. "Nothing compared to you, genius. There. 11. Break the seal and open it up. Once the fog dissipates, use the stim shot and the adrenaline."

"Well, the shot is no problem, but how do I use this thing?" Cary asked, holding up the cylinder of adrenaline.

Ryne picked up his, hit a button on the end so that a sharp, thick needle sprang out. "You jam it in the chest it auto-injects into the heart." Cary just stared at him in horror. "Jesus, Cary, you computer-engineer viral DNA that changes the makeup of the human body and brain. How can this bother you?"

Cary just shook his head. "Makes me think how far overboard we've gone," he murmured. "You don't jam hulking needles into V3s. They have ports."

Ryne's water-blue eyes met Cary's green ones for a long moment before they both looked away, uncomfortable. Ryne nodded and turned back to the computer and Cary looked over his shoulder again. "Hypervascular, hyperfocus, specialty: munitions; handle: 'Brimstone'," Cary read off.

"Bay 3," Ryne murmured, picking up the stim and cylinder and limping around the room. Cary went the opposite direction. Finding the bays, they both keyed them open and popped the seals. The hiss of air sounded loud in the metal-wrapped room and the white, cold fog that drifted out was dry instead of ice-wet.

A panel slid open and the biobed slid out of the wall as the cryo fog fizzed and melted away, exposing the body. Electrodes ran from the bed to the V1's face and neck, flashing slowly. Cary looked down at the soldier dressed in black uniform trousers and a tank top, which exposed his shoulders and arms. He was muscled, but not obscenely so like the V3s. His face was chiseled and his hair was dark and a little overgrown; it stood out against pale skin. He looked like your typical military grunt, but coldly handsome, like a statue carved from marble. Cary slid the needle into the crook of his arm and gave him the stim, then swallowed as he expelled the needle on the adrenaline.

Ryne opened his bay, watching the narrow table slide out and the fog lift. The electrodes blinked on the V1's forehead, drawing Ryne's attention to a scruffy face with full lips and a widow's peak. As it was, rough was the best description Ryne could come up with. The tank exposed lean, muscled arms and a wiry build. He handily administered the stim, pulled the tank free of the waistband, and rucked it up to reveal a surprisingly hairless chest, dog tags and a LCD chip. Pushing the tags out of the way, he raised the cylinder over the soldier's heart.

Cary took a breath, moved the tank and the dog tags, and jammed the cylinder down hard. The thick needle drove deep and the adrenaline shot out, and before he could even step back the V1 jerked straight up with a sharp gasp of a breath, his hands clutching his chest.

Distracted by the noise, Ryne glanced over to see Cary standing next to the V1 he'd just awakened. The soldier was working hard to breathe and the cylinder hit the floor as he jerked it right out of his chest. Ryne looked back at the soldier on the table in front of him, curled his fist around the cylinder and jammed it down. He stumbled back, trying to favor his hurt leg when the man shot straight up choking for air after a matter of heartbeats.

"Ryne..." Cary said shakily as the V1 in front of him started into convulsions, falling back on the biobed. He was shaking so hard that Cary could barely keep him on the table.

"Don't let him fall!" Ryne yelled. The soldier in front of him was curled over on himself, shivering as his tags hung loose, swinging. Although not sure what to do, Ryne couldn't stand to see the cylinder and needle bobbing in his chest, so he reached over and pulled it out – and one very strong hand flashed out to grab his wrist in a painfully tight hold.

Cary had his arms around the V1, trying to hold him still, when suddenly the soldier sat up again, throwing Cary so off balance that he stumbled back several steps. It was a good thing... the soldier vomited clear liquid violently over the edge of the bed and finally relaxed, panting.

Ryne stared at the glazed hazel eyes that gave the V1 much more personality than he had expected. They were real eyes, shockingly full of life, even filled with understandable confusion, not flat, unmoving discs. He tried to pull his wrist out of the solid grip, but there was no way. "It's okay," he said calmly, hoping the soldier understood him. Sometimes cryo left your brain a little frozen at first. The V1 blinked hard several times, still struggling for breath, and after a long pause seemed to make a decision. He let go of Ryne's wrist, letting his hand drop back to the edge of the bed. Ryne started pulling off electrodes, trying not to jar the man overmuch. Shoulders bowed, the soldier's breathing started to calm, and eyes that glittered with intelligence looked up at Ryne. The V1 tried to speak, but apparently his throat was too dry.

"I'm sorry, we don't have anything here. This was sort of... an emergency," Ryne said.

The man looked at him hard for a long moment and then moved, slinging his legs over the side so bare feet slapped onto the cold floor. Ryne leaned back against the wall of bays just in time to avoid being knocked over as the soldier slowly straightened his shoulders and started looking around, leaning heavily on the biobed.

Ryne watched as the soldier got to his feet, regaining his balance, obviously surveying the room until his eyes settled on the other V1 and Cary. When he tried to speak this time a raspy growl came out. "Nighthawk."

The other V1 stirred and shifted, pushing himself up to look across the room in acknowledgment. Cary watched the other soldier stand and almost collapse, catching the bed in time, which made him look back at the V1 in front of him. Now that there was life and color back in his face, the scientist could see clearly where the code name came from: black hair, dark as night, and a sharp, angled face. Then the man's eyes opened. They were dark, dark brown and immediately calculating. Cary and Ryne watched, cautious. Cary wondered if they were going to die. Ryne wondered if they were going to live.

Nighthawk groaned and shoved his legs off the bed to stand, holding onto the edge as he got his feet. His voice was mangled, too. "What's up, Brimstone?"

"Emergency," Brimstone rasped, and his gaze swung about to pin on Ryne. "Profile?" the V1 asked.

"Profile?" Ryne echoed, brow furrowing.

"He wants to know what's going on, Ryne," Cary said. "A profile of the situation."

"Oh. Situation," Ryne looked back at Brimstone. "The command in this facility plans to use the military made up of Spec 4 V3s to declare martial law, take over the country, and start eliminating all unengineered humans."

Cary paled. He'd had no idea of the scope of what was happening. "*Jesus*, Ryne..."

Brimstone just stared at him silently, as did Nighthawk. Then they looked at each other, and Brimstone slowly raised a hand to rub it across his face. "I should have retired," he muttered.

"You had your chance, you bastard," Nighthawk said with a thick chuckle, now standing straight, rubbing at where the needle had pierced his chest.

"Fuck you, pretty boy," Brimstone snarled back.

"Anytime," Nighthawk chuckled, leaning back against the bed, actually smiling.

Cary and Ryne just stared.


THE scientist and the engineer ran down the hall, trying to keep up with Nighthawk while Brimstone stalked a ways behind them, keeping an eye on the hallways they passed. "Who the hell are these guys?" Cary asked for about the tenth time.

"Cary, will you *shut up* about it? You want to live through this or not?" Ryne hissed.

"How do we know they won't just kill us and go join the V3s?"

"Because we're still human."

The two men stopped in place, almost running right into Nighthawk. "We're still human, and from what you just briefed us, *they* never were," the soldier said. "They won't accept us. That's why we were put on ice in the first place. For the new wave of soldiers to move in."

Brimstone walked past them, face set in a permanent frown. "Get moving," he said in a clipped voice.

So they followed Brimstone now, moving as quickly as they could down the passageway, considering Ryne's injured leg. "Why didn't they just kill you?" Ryne asked over his shoulder.

"Commit mass murder? Wasn't quite possible. So they put us away for 'just in case', you know? Me, I was just me, so I really didn't care. Happy to still be breathing. Or not breathing, as the case was," Nighthawk answered frankly. "But alive."

"So why's he so pissed off?" Cary asked, nodding his head at the soldier stalking ahead of them.

The V1 didn't answer right away as they moved down the hallway. His movements were silent on his bare feet and when he did speak, it was just as quietly. "He left a family behind."

Ryne frowned. "How long have you guys been in there?"

"What year is it?" Nighthawk asked as they turned a corner. Brimstone was most of the way up the passage already.

"2085," Cary said.

Nighthawk stopped in his tracks and looked back at them, his dark eyes clearly shocked. "I thought cryo was only good for twenty years max," he hissed.

"Yes, that's right," Ryne said, frowning as they stopped. "The other eight in the bays were dead." He looked over Nighthawk's shoulder after Brimstone, but the other V1 hadn't stopped. He was now checking doors.

"We were put down in '28," Nighthawk said angrily. "They said ten years, at the most, then we'd be processed out as civilians. Fuck..." Now he turned and looked after Brimstone. "All dead. He's gonna be pissed."

Both of Cary's brows flew up. "And how is that a difference from now?" he asked, voice nearing strident. "Guys, we better get down there or the pissing will start now instead of later," he said, pushing them to start back up the hall as the scruffy V1 looked toward them, scowling. They caught up with him at a nondescript sealed door.

"Open it," Brimstone ordered.

Ryne took one look at his face and tried a couple codes. The third one opened the door and Brimstone strode inside. The other men followed and when the lights flickered on, Cary turned in a circle. "Armory," he identified.

"Pft," Nighthawk dismissed, already rifling a clothes locker. "Brimstone's gotta have his guns to get his rocks off."

"Shut your trap, asshole."

"Sure thing, Brimstone," Nighthawk said back, voice bright and shiny.

"You guys are something else," Cary said as he sat on a bench, watching Ryne wander farther back in the room.

Nighthawk pulled out black jackets, web gear and more. "Here, put on these." He tossed a set of trousers and shirt like his own at Cary, hitting him in the chest.

"What for? These are V3 uniforms."

"Really? Even better."

"Why better? I don't want to look like one of them," Cary objected.

"You want a hole in your leg like Ryne's?"

"I'll just go change now."

"There's a jacket and more," Nighthawk said, shrugging into the gear himself and pulling out boots.

Ryne stopped some distance away from Brimstone as the V1 shoved through a locker. "What are we going to do?" he asked.

Brimstone's eyes shifted to him. They were cold, but even so, they still had much more life than a V3's. "First, we're going to remove the noncombatants from the zone. Second, we'll infiltrate the facility's substructure and eliminate the central command. Third, we'll find the V3 nerve case and blow it. That sound okay to you?" His last words were clearly sarcastic.

"As long as the command center is taken out. Like I said, that's where they're coordinating everything from. But destroying the nerve case, that would decimate the entire military," Ryne said, a little shocked.

"You want the V3s to run the country?" Brimstone said sharply.

"No!"

"Then we take out the nerve case or this'll be happening again in a year and you won't be around to get someone to do something about it." Brimstone closed the few steps between them and reached down to grab Ryne's torn-up leg. The redhead yelped and tried to jerk away. "If what you said tracks, when that V3 cut you up, it took a tissue sample. It will know you, wherever you are, wherever you go. That's standard fluid and tissue tracking. There's no escaping it unless the whole damn thing is taken down." He released Ryne's leg and stalked back to the locker. "Should never have gone up in the first place," he muttered.

Ryne watched the dark man shrug into a heavy jacket and wrap belts around his chest and waist before sliding into boots. The V1 moved with an economy of motion that captivated him. It reminded him of what he'd read on the computer. "Your specialty is munitions. That's why you wanted the armory," Ryne said, making the connection.

Brimstone's chin jerked around. "You read my file?"

"I was looking for someone to help us. I knew military would be the best bet, but it had to be military that wouldn't really know what's been going on." Ryne shrugged apologetically. "Luckily, I stumbled across some old records about the deep freeze. We got Nighthawk, then you."

Jaw shifting, Brimstone frowned. "What about the rest of my team?"

Ryne shut his mouth, inhaled sharply through his nose and swallowed on it. "They're dead. The cryo failed. It's been far too long. It's amazing that the two of you are still alive."

The little bit of life in the V1's eyes went out, replaced by implacable focus. "Put these on," he said roughly, shoving a black V3 uniform against Ryne's chest.

Wandering into the washroom, Nighthawk walked up behind Cary, who stood in front of a small mirror mounted on a locker. "This isn't going to work," the soldier said, pulling on Cary's platinum tail of hair. "Not exactly regulation."

"Can't do anything about it," Cary said, pulling off his glasses and sliding them into a pocket.

"I can," Nighthawk said, pulling a sharp knife out of an arm sheath. Before Cary could protest, the knife sheared close to the scalp through his hair, and Nighthawk held the tail out to him.

Cary blinked at the hair, then back up at the mirror. "Great," he muttered.

Nighthawk grinned and reached up to cut some of the sides so it tapered messily close to his skull. "That'll pass muster."

Cary rolled his eyes. "I guess I'll just grow it out again. If I live through this," he said sarcastically.

"Oh, I don't know," Nighthawk purred, leaning close and sniffing delicately along the line of Cary's neck. "I like it short." His lips just barely brushed along the bared neck and Cary shivered, eyes widening.

Grinning because he wasn't pushed away, Nighthawk slid his hands onto Cary's waist. "Don't worry. I'll make sure you live," he murmured, smiling against Cary's ear. "You're kinda cute."

Cary couldn't stifle the snort. "Gee. Cute. Thanks."

"I like cute," Nighthawk said, setting his chin on Cary's shoulder, nuzzling his neck.

"You wake up randy?" Cary poked.

"Mmmm hmmm," Nighthawk answered, rubbing against him from behind.

Cary laughed. "Your sense of reality is so skewed."

"Mmmm baby, let me rock your world."

Ryne turned to look back into the room as Cary's laughter echoed around them, but he and Nighthawk weren't in sight. He glanced back when Brimstone snorted. "What?"

"Nighthawk never could keep it in his pants," the V1 muttered. Ryne's brows hit the ceiling. Brimstone glanced at him and shrugged. "Try this jacket," he said, holding one out.

Ryne accepted it and slid it on, fastening the web belt, sending another odd glance in the direction of the washroom. Brimstone looked over it and reached to tighten the jacket around him, pulling on the straps around his chest and waist. "Not too tight?" he asked gruffly.

"No, it's fine," Ryne answered, looking at the dog tags and chip swinging across Brimstone's chest. The soldier turned away and tucked the tags into his tank before pulling on a jacket himself. "How are we going to do this?" Ryne asked.

"There is no 'we' — you're leaving," Brimstone said in a clipped voice.

"Leaving? I'm not leaving. What are you talking about?" Ryne asked in shock.

Brimstone slammed the door shut and turned on him. "You. Are. Leaving." Then he stalked back toward the door.

"You can't do this without me," Ryne objected, following him.

"Watch me," Brimstone said succinctly. "Nighthawk," he barked. "Zip it up and get out here."

After a long moment the other V1 sauntered into the main room. "Are we ready to party?"

"Arm up," Brimstone said.

"You can't do this without me," Ryne insisted as Cary walked out, flushed and smoothing a hand over his shorn head. Ryne did a double take before looking back at the grim soldier.

"Why not?" Nighthawk asked as he pulled a large gun off a weapons rack and handed it to Brimstone.

"Because I have all the pass codes," Ryne said, straightening his shoulders. Nighthawk raised one brow and looked from the scientist to the other V1 and back. Then he started whistling quietly, turned right around, took Cary's arm and walked him into the washroom.

"Wha..." Cary said.

"Trust me," Nighthawk said, pulling him around the corner and starting to grope again. "This will be much less violent."

"You have no experience for this mission," Brimstone grated as he sat on the bench and started working on the gun.

"But I've got all the knowledge you don't," Ryne argued, crossing his arms and standing in front of the soldier. "It won't work without both components."

The V1s eyes narrowed. "You're a doctor, aren't you." It wasn't a question.

"I'm a geneticist, yes."

"So you know what makes the V3s tick?"

"I know about the genetic and biological components. You'd have to ask Cary about the actual programming," Ryne said, voice revealing his unease. "What do you need to know?"

"I need to know what we're up against. Obviously, I only know the bare bits you've told us about the V3s, plus a few rumors from before I went under." Brimstone grimaced. "This is not a good idea," he muttered.

"Yeah, well, the whole situation is fucked, so I don't know what to tell you," Ryne muttered, sitting down and wiping sweat off his brow. His cheeks were a little flushed and he fanned himself with one hand.

"How did a scientist find out about this plot, anyway?" the soldier asked suspiciously as he pulled another gun of the rack next to where he sat.

"Rise in percentages of genetically engineered components in the V3s without them being expressly planned. Drop in averages of genetic adjustments in the general population. Higher causal deaths in nonengineered population." Brimstone looked at Ryne like he was spouting another language. Ryne sighed. "I'm also a numbers cruncher. I know what improvements are being used on the V3s, and more were showing up than I had records for. They were being made stronger, less instinctual, more highly programmed with artificial intelligence instead of genetic knowledge. They're practically machines now."

Brimstone's eyes were clouded as he looked across the room. "Do they carry the same enhancements the V1s did?" he asked, practically cordial.

Ryne shook his head, tilting his head as he studied Brimstone's closed face. "A lot of the early genetic manipulations went bad in V2. The engineering that took in V1s mutated in V2s and the entire project fell apart. That run was scrapped and the V3s were designed from the ground up."

"So it's been how long since anyone's dealt with a V1?" Brimstone asked, still staring off at nothing.

"Fifty years, give or take. I'd never even seen the research until I started looking for more information. I had no idea that the subjects were even created. I'd been told V1 was all lab work. Even with my knowledge, I didn't understand most of what they did to V1s. And most of the research was wiped from the database. The only reason I found your bays was an old maintenance order."

Brimstone's face got pinched. "Fifty years," he murmured. "So how do we take out the V3s?"

"I don't know about you guys, but Cary and I are no match for them. The strength is incredible. Guns work – the V3s are still primarily flesh and blood except for the brain and cybernetic components in joints and such," Ryne explained, leaning back against the lockers. "But the nerve case is really what keeps them going. Without the transmitted programming they shut down and the clean up sequence starts."

"What's that?" Brimstone asked, grabbing yet another weapon.

"Basal conflagration decomposition. The components burn themselves out and consume the body within one hour. It was conceived as a way to keep the battlefields cleaned up."

The V1 set aside the gun and leaned on his knees, looking across at Ryne in a clearly measuring way, seeing the scientist's athletic build only emphasized by the uniform. He was obviously a book man, but perhaps not so useless, or helpless, as Brimstone had initially judged. "Are the people in the command center human or engineered?"

Ryne was thrown by the jump, but after a moment his face filled with an ill grief. "Human, maybe five percent engineered, like the general population," he said quietly as his eyes dropped to his fists. "Megalomaniacs, but human."

"Why are you doing this?" Brimstone asked, his voice gentle enough to draw Ryne's gaze back to the soldier's face and his changeable eyes. The soldier knew well enough how difficult it was to come to terms with having to kill.

"What they're doing is wrong," Ryne answered, a hint of steel in his voice. "Engineering was meant to improve the human race, remove disease and defects, extend age and improve quality of life. Not to make a superior master race."

Brimstone studied him and then nodded slowly. "You listen to me when we're out there, you understand? I'll do my best to get you out of this, but I think we both know this is bigger than any of us and has to be stopped."

The scientist raised his chin. "Yeah. It has to be stopped."

THEY walked calmly down the corridor, Nighthawk first, comm fixed firmly in his ear. Cary and Ryne followed side by side with Brimstone bringing up the rear. Hide in plain sight, Nighthawk had suggested. Blow their way in, Brimstone had suggested. He was outvoted. And he was annoyed as all hell, but going along with it. Stoically.

"Is this gonna work?" Ryne muttered.

"Yes. It's going to work," Cary answered automatically, tinkering with a handheld comp pad they'd filched from an admin office.

"You sound so sure," Ryne said sharply.

"Shut it," was growled from behind them.

Nighthawk stopped and stiffened. "Someone's around the corner," he said quietly.

Ryne frowned. "I don't hear anything."

Brimstone hushed him and nodded. "Go, Nighthawk."

The V1 headed down the hall soundlessly, and the two men watched with wide eyes; he was nearly forty feet away at the end of the hall before they blinked. Cary glanced to Brimstone with wide eyes. "What the hell?" he whispered. The V1 just shook his head as Nighthawk disappeared around a corner.

Within a minute, Nighthawk stuck his head around the corner and gestured for them to follow. They came around the corner and stopped. Two V3s lay on the floor, prone, twisted into odd shapes. Cary stopped and stared, and Ryne had to nudge him along. Brimstone just stepped over the bodies and up to the door. "Key code," he told Ryne with a sharp toss of his head.

The scientist approached the key pad and got the door open. They all moved inside and Nighthawk and Brimstone dragged the bodies in after them.

"Nighthawk?" Cary asked. "What..."

"Don't ask about what you don't want to know," Nighthawk said seriously, dark eyes meeting blue ones when they looked up from the body. Ryne squeezed Cary's shoulder in silent support and walked after Brimstone, who was moving to a console of computer screens.

"I'll need a few minutes," the engineer murmured as he plugged the pad into the computer and sat to start typing. After a moment, lines of complex code scrolled down the screens.

"What is that?" Brimstone asked, leaning over Cary's shoulder.

"Computer DNA," Cary said absently.

"You're some kind of computer geek?" Nighthawk asked.

"He's *the* computer geek," Ryne said as he watched the lines of code skim down the screen in indecipherable patterns. "He designed most of the programming in the current engineering initiatives."

"Right smart little prodigy, isn't he?" Nighthawk said with a grin. He leaned over Cary's shoulder as Ryne accessed a different computer a few feet away. "So. Just how smart are we?" he asked.

Cary's eyes shifted to him, then back to the code. "Off the scale," he answered. "Before enhancement."

Nighthawk whistled quietly. "That's some brain you got in there," he said, knocking his knuckles lightly on Cary's skull.

"Yeah, it comes in handy, I guess," the engineer said as he typed quickly.

"I never was one for books so much. Actions, that's me," the V1 said casually.

"Somehow I doubt that means you're not of above average intelligence," Cary said in a pointed tone.

"Hmmm, well, I hold my own," Nighthawk replied modestly.

Cary smiled, never looking away from the monitor. "Yeah. You do." The V1 grinned.

Ryne pulled up the schematics they needed. "I found it," he said to Brimstone.

The soldier moved to his side. "One level down, storage room 4F," he said while fixing the map firmly in mind.

"Should be enough explosives there for two rooms the size of the case," Ryne noted. "Remotes too."

"Yeah, well, we don't intend to set them off while we're in the room," Brimstone said with a hint of a smile.

Ryne glanced up, a grin hovering around the corners of his lips. "Did you just crack a joke?"

"Get your hearing checked," Brimstone answered, looking across the room at nothing in particular. But the smile was still there.

"I thought maybe you'd traded your sense of humor for an enhancement," Ryne teased.

Brimstone's lips twitched. "Thought about it," he admitted.

"You think too much, Brimstone," Nighthawk said from the other side of Cary.

"And you think too little, Nighthawk," the V1 retorted.

"Sure I think. Just not always with the same head," Nighthawk snarked.

Ryne snickered as Brimstone rolled his eyes. "How is it you two are so different? The V3s are practically carbon copies."

"This one's just naturally got a stick up his ass," Nighthawk poked at his fellow V1.

"Better than your cock; no telling where it's been," Brimstone shot back. Hands covering his heart, Nighthawk mimed stumbling, a pained look on his face.

Amused, Ryne shook his head. But a question was bothering him. "Nighthawk, despite what you said, I want to know. How did you do that out in the hall? They were top line V3s. They should have wiped the passageway with you."

Nighthawk glanced to Brimstone, who just returned his look expressionlessly. "Would you believe me if I said it was the human factor?" Nighthawk asked, crossing his arms. Cary glanced up from the keyboard to listen.

The scientist frowned. "What makes you human would logically make you weaker," he said hesitantly.

"Physically, maybe. But not mentally. Not at all," Nighthawk said.

"They don't think," Brimstone said quietly. "They react based on factored parameters. They can't adjust on the fly or make split-second changes."

Ryne frowned. "So you took them out by being unpredictable?"

Nighthawk grinned. "That's me," he said. "Unpredictable." Brimstone snorted from where he leaned against the console, cradling one of his guns.

"And fast," Cary murmured as his fingers went back to clattering on the keyboard.

Ryne glanced between the V1s. Nighthawk looked again to Brimstone, whose lips twitched. "And fast?" Ryne asked.

"One of my enhancements," Nighthawk said. "Increased muscular reaction and synapse control." And again he looked to Brimstone.

"Is he holding your leash?" the redhead finally asked him with a huff.

"In a manner of speaking," Brimstone rumbled. Nighthawk just waggled his eyebrows. But neither of them elaborated.

Cary stopped typing and looked over his shoulder, remembering how easily Nighthawk had lifted him and held him against a wall. "And strength? Those V3s can bench press a small tank." Nighthawk just shrugged, which drew a soft bark of laughter from Brimstone.

"When have you ever been modest?" the scruffy V1 asked in mock disbelief. Nighthawk stuck his tongue out at him.

"You two are close," Ryne observed.

Brimstone's slight smirk faded. "We all were," he said quietly.

"The ten of us worked, ate, slept and breathed together for five years, learning how to mesh our enhancements to make the best team," Nighthawk explained, a note of upset creeping into his voice. "I feel like I've lost most of my limbs."

Ryne let the conversation drop as Cary got back to the code. After a few quiet minutes, the engineer stopped again. "Okay, I've taken out the security directives surrounding the command center, disabled the outgoing call lines, jammed the command codes to weapons lockers and locked down the bulkhead doors. But I can't access the nerve core to stop response measures. They'd notice immediately."

"Score one for the geek," Nighthawk drawled, patting Cary's shoulder.

"Better than what we had," Brimstone said. He shifted his weapon to his opposite arm and pulled a compact handgun from a shoulder holster. "Take this," the V1 said, holding it out to Ryne. "Need me to show you how to use it?"

Ryne reached out and took the gun, sighed, checked the ammunition clip and chamber handily, and stuck the gun in his waistband. Brimstone watched, question clear. "Can't be too careful," Ryne said. "A lot has changed out in the world while you've been asleep."

Cary joined them, bringing the comm pad. Nighthawk bumped his shoulder. "You want a gun?"

"I wouldn't know what to do with a gun," Cary said. "I'll stick to these." He reached in the leg pocket of his uniform and held up several sedative shots.

"So that's what you were loading up back in the cryo lab," Ryne said as he wiped at his forehead and shifted uncomfortably. Cary nodded.

"Everybody clear on the plan?" Brimstone asked. The other three men agreed. As they made for the door, the V1 put one hand on Ryne's shoulder. "How's the leg?" he asked quietly.

Ryne turned his chin. "Hurts like hell," he muttered. "Let's go. Sooner we're done, sooner I'm off it."

Their progress to the command center was unimpeded, though Nighthawk's warnings increased in number and there were a couple close calls. Using a gesture, Brimstone sent Nighthawk to the other side of the metal doors and checked the gun in his hands one more time. As he met the other men's eyes, they heard footsteps approaching from a side hallway. It was now or never.

Nighthawk hit the key code and Brimstone was inside in the next breath, his gun chattering and choking. Cary and Ryne ducked and ran around the door frame to the inside of the room, wincing as other single shots bounced around the room. Nighthawk followed them, closing and locking the door, then sped across the room to intercept the V3 guards moving in their direction.

Knowing their goals, Cary and Ryne split up to sabotage the computers, crouching below the screens as they worked, listening to the yells and spatter of gunfire striking metal with loud pings and sinking into bodies with soft thuds. Ryne pulled two chunks of explosive out of his chest pockets and pressed them underneath the consoles, sliding remote tabs into them.

"Brimstone, watch your six," Nighthawk barked, his smooth spinning jump ramming his booted heel into a V3's jaw, snapping its neck and dropping it.

The other V1 snapped around and took out the lieutenants with handguns, easy targets. But his attention was drawn to the back of the room as V3s were prying open the magnetically sealed door with their bare hands. "Time to go," Brimstone stated firmly, hurrying over to the console where Cary was working.

"Almost," Cary said frantically.

Nighthawk ducked incoming fire as the V3s stuck a gun muzzle through the partially opened door and strafed the room. Brimstone hunched down to avoid the hail of bullets, snapped a setting on the gun, stood, aimed and fired – the single bullet zeroed right through the two-inch crack to take out the V3 handling the gun.

He heard the trigger pull behind him and moved, but he wasn't fast enough.

"Brimstone!" Ryne yelled as the V1 took several shots right in the chest and gut from an injured captain who'd drawn a sidearm. Staggering backward, Brimstone's hands closed over his belly, and he fell over and hit the floor hard as Nighthawk cleared the tall console in an athletic leap and practically took the captain's head off with one kick.

Cary stood up from where he'd crouched behind the other console. "Nighthawk, they're coming through," he yelled, pointing at the back door that was now being pulled open, the metal scraping and protesting but giving in under the massive strength of combined V3s. With a grunt, Nighthawk moved and lifted a broken piece of plastisteel table, hurling it at the door, smashing the two V3s trying to enter. The bodies were dispassionately pushed out of the way as more V3s worked to get in.

"Time to move," Nighthawk said calmly, walking over and picking Brimstone up, throwing his limp body over his shoulder. "Cary, the escape route?"

The engineer ran across the room and behind a fake wall, opening an access tube that led away from the command center. He scrambled inside the four-foot around passageway and Ryne followed. "Mission completed?" Nighthawk asked as he crawled in and dragged the other V1 in behind him.

"Yeah," Ryne said, breaths harsh as he looked at the still V1.

"Move," Nighthawk hissed, and Cary led the way through the tube until they reached the crossing and turned. "Now, Ryne."

The scientist pressed a button on the small box in his hand and they heard a muffled explosion and then a huge rush of air. The tube shuddered around them. "Get moving," Nighthawk instructed. He dragged Brimstone by the collar as he followed them.


NIGHTHAWK carried Brimstone over to a cot in the long-unused lab and carefully laid him down while Ryne watched, outwardly horrified. Nighthawk's eyes flickered to the scientist, but the V1 didn't say anything as he walked over to a cabinet and rifled through it.

Ryne limped toward the cot and stopped beside it, looking down at the face that was as pale and lifeless as when he'd first seen it in cryo. He covered his stinging eyes, rubbing at them. What would they do now? Nighthawk was still a positive in their favor, but without Brimstone, what chance would they have? Letting out a shuddering sigh, he looked back down at Brimstone, whose hazel eyes were watching him.

"Holy shit!" Ryne yelled, jumping back in shock.

Several feet away, Nighthawk snickered, and an equally surprised Cary thwapped him in the chest with the comm pad.

"What the *hell*?" Ryne said loudly as Brimstone sat up with a groan.

"You know, I think sometimes that's an awfully handy enhancement to have. But then I always think, damn, that must hurt," Nighthawk said as if nothing were wrong.

"Hurts like hell," Brimstone muttered, poking his chest carefully.

"Enhancement? What kind of enhancement does that?" Cary asked in disbelief.

"Super healing," Nighthawk said buoyantly.

"Bullshit," Brimstone snapped, face clenched in pain. "Body protects itself, that's all. Expels foreign objects." Ryne stood there, speechless.

"And heals itself super fast," Nighthawk confided to Cary in a stage whisper.

"You didn't think to share this with the rest of us?" Cary asked, now decidedly annoyed. "I think Ryne had a damn stroke. I know I had a heart attack when I saw you go down."

"Would you have believed me?" Brimstone asked as he shifted his legs off the cot to carefully sit upright. He looked up at Ryne, taking note of the anguished look on his face, and had to look away.

Cary shuffled to one side as Nighthawk pushed past him with bandages. "No, I guess not," the engineer murmured.

Nighthawk helped Brimstone pull off his web gear, jacket, and tank, the smashed bullets falling to the floor with dull tings as they shook loose of the fabric, leaving bloody rents in the flesh. Brimstone winced as Nighthawk pressed the gauze against them, and Ryne watched as the skin closed in on itself and sealed the wounds. The V1 hissed, his hands gripping the edge of the cot tightly.

"Ya big baby," Nighthawk muttered.

"Go fuck yourself," Brimstone growled.

"I'm flexible, but not that flexible," Nighthawk said with a chuckle. After another minute he added, "All right, bad boy, they're all closed up. Any more?"

Brimstone winced and nodded, leaning back and pushing at the waistband of the trousers. Nighthawk unfastened them and pulled the fabric away, letting a handful of shot ping and scatter on the floor, revealing the messy, crimson mess of the V1's gut.

"*Damnit*, Brimstone," Nighthawk whined. "You know how much I hate looking at this kind of shit." The other soldier cuffed him upside the head. "Fuck, all right... Ryne, I need more gauze," he said.

The scientist didn't move, so Cary grabbed the box and brought it over to the cot. When he glanced up, Ryne looked really shaky. "C'mon Ryne, let's go find a place to rest. I don't know about you, but I'm exhausted." Ryne let Cary lead him across the room to another cot, where he sat down hard, grabbing his leg.

"Wish he hadn't had to see that, but I couldn't stand it anymore," Brimstone muttered as he flinched under the gauze, gritting his teeth as his body knitted itself back together.

"You old softy," Nighthawk teased, dabbing at the wounds as they closed up. His voice was serious when he locked their gazes and spoke again. "You got to be more careful. This one was bad."

"Yeah," Brimstone breathed. "I know."

Nighthawk nodded. Looking down, he saw clear, unblemished skin. "All healed up," he said, lightly slapping Brimstone's belly as he stood up.

"Mother fucker!" Brimstone hissed, kicking out at him, but Nighthawk jumped out of the way too fast. "*Son of a bitch*," the hurting V1 cursed as he fastened his pants and pushed himself back up to sit.

Grinning, Nighthawk sauntered across the room to catch up with Cary, grabbed hold of his web gear, and practically dragged him into the next lab after whispering in his ear.

"This so isn't the time or place," Cary breathed as Nighthawk sealed the door and pushed him against the wall with his body.

"Always the time and place," Nighthawk argued, dipping his head to lick along Cary's jaw. "Never know if there'll be another," he pointed out. "Might as well get it when you can."

"God... Do you fuck everyone who comes along?" Cary asked as he shivered in Nighthawk's arms.

"Nah. Just the cute blond ones," the V1 answered, unfastening the front of Cary's jacket.

"So I'm just lucky then," Cary said, his hands moving to uncover Nighthawk's chest.

"Hmmm. Something more than lucky," Nighthawk growled as he pulled at the fastenings to Cary's trousers. The engineer shimmied to help, which made Nighthawk freeze and groan. "You're gonna have to tell me if I get too rough," he said raggedly, stepping back to push his own pants down while Cary pulled a tube of lotion from his pocket, gleaned from the washroom at the armory.

Cary nodded, getting some lotion in his hand and cupping Nighthawk's erection. "I'll tell you. Now fuck me."

Nighthawk growled again and spun Cary around, pushing his legs apart as far as they would go with the pants around his ankles. His own were around his lower thighs as he bent his knees enough to get the right angle to push inside with a hard thrust.

"Fuck yes!" Cary howled before Nighthawk covered his mouth with one hand as he drilled into him precisely.

"Can't make too much noise," the V1 panted. "Don't want Brimstone comin' in to kick the shit out of us for giving away our position."

Cary whimpered and pushed his hips back, trying to participate. The soldier lowered his forehead to Cary's shoulder and kept moving, one hand curled about the engineer's waist to keep him from ramming into the wall as the thrusts got progressively harder. Cary shouted encouragement against Nighthawk's thick fingers, his own hand frantically pumping himself.

"C'mon, baby," Nighthawk crooned in Cary's ear. "Give daddy some sugar..." When Cary thrashed as his climax hit him, Nighthawk stiffened, frozen deep inside Cary's body, and shuddered, hips shifting slightly with each pulse, egged on by the contractions from his lover.

In the lab next door, Brimstone lurched to his feet with a heartfelt groan, pulling the torn up tank back on and shrugging into the jacket, though he left it hanging open. "Ryne?" he said tentatively as he crossed the lab.

The scientist was leaning against the wall, exhaustion and near-agony written in his hunched shoulders and grasping hands. "Yeah," he answered raggedly, eyes still shut.

"You look about as bad as me," Brimstone said as he walked over to stand beside him.

Ryne sighed and pried open his eyes to look up at the V1. "I could use some of that super healing about now," he said weakly.

Brimstone frowned. "Your leg?" He crouched down to look at where Ryne clutched his upper thigh, and a light touch of his fingertips came away bloody. "Hell," he muttered. With a smooth motion he stood and grabbed the First Aid kit Nighthawk had found.

"It's bad," Ryne murmured.

"Are you a doctor now?" Brimstone asked sarcastically as he knelt down with the kit.

"Actually, yes, I am," Ryne said, laughing a little tightly. "Physiology and surgery, before I specialized in genetics."

"Well, lucky then, aren't you?" Brimstone said as he pulled a utility knife out of his belt and sliced the trouser leg open to reveal the dark copper-soaked bandage. "How'd you stay up on this thing?"

"Sheer will and adrenaline."

"Sure you're not enhanced?" the soldier asked as he carefully pulled the wet gauze away.

"Not with healing," Ryne admitted, wincing as the slop of gauze pulled away from the inflamed gouge. "Your enhancement is... amazing. I've never seen anything like it. I wouldn't even have conceived designing it."

"Yeah, well, it's not all it's cracked up to be," Brimstone muttered as he prodded at the somewhat closed gash.

Ryne hissed in pain and lurched to the side. "Go over there to the cabinet and get a dissection kit," he ordered in a shaky voice.

Brimstone looked up sharply. "Ryne..."

"Do it. I have to be able to walk," the scientist insisted.

The soldier found the box and returned, ripping the end off the package. "You want something to bite down on?" he asked seriously.

Ryne shook his head. "I can't imagine how it could hurt more," he mumbled. "Do it." He wrapped his fingers around the metal bars that held up the cot and took a couple even breaths.

After a long look at the scientist, Brimstone picked up the scalpel, grasped Ryne's leg to hold it as still as possible, and steadily but quickly sliced through the stiff skin and scab covering the wound. It popped open, a bubble of yellow and black infection letting loose and mixing heavily with blood. Brimstone carefully wiped it away, glancing up at Ryne's white face. He was trembling, and his breathing was sharp and shallow.

"Get that shit out," he whispered, and Brimstone started squeezing the sides of the gash, pausing when Ryne passed out and went limp. The soldier kept working the wound, pushing out more pus and dirt until the blood ran as clear as he could get it. Drawing a breath, he poured antiseptic right into the torn skin. Ryne jerked and came awake with a fractured cry of agony. The V1 slathered antibiotic cream over it and wrapped it up best he could before shooting the scientist up with a large syringe of painkillers and antibiotics.

"Jesus fucking Christ," Ryne hissed.

The soldier looked up at the suffering man, respect and compassion clear on his face. "You did good, doc," he said quietly.

Ryne whimpered, breathless with pain as his eyes rolled. "I'll pass on a repeat. Oh God..."

Brimstone pushed the kit to clatter to the floor and sat on the cot, pulling Ryne up against him. "'s okay," he murmured as the man shifted to huddle under his arm.

"Now you act like a nice guy," Ryne muttered against his jacket, hand curled into the open jacket.

The V1 chuckled. "Now you've earned it."

After being silent for several long minutes, enclosed in Brimstone's arms, the scientist shuddered. "I thought you were dead."

The V1 turned his chin and pressed a chaste kiss to Ryne's forehead. "Takes more than that to kill me."

"Thank God," Ryne said fervently, drawing a wry smile from the soldier. His voice got quieter. "I like you like this."

Brimstone sighed. "Gotta turn it off when I'm working," he said neutrally.

"And now?"

"Not working now," the V1 murmured, lowering his chin to nuzzle Ryne's temple, making him shiver and tip his head back. Brimstone studied his eyes for a long moment before dipping to kiss him lightly once, twice before Ryne pushed closer and sealed their lips together.

Their mouths slid warm and wet against each other as the kiss went on. Ryne finally pull back to suck in a breath, and Brimstone's hands began to roam, eliciting a soft moan.

"Hurting?" the V1 asked quietly. His eyes were closed as he held the scientist against him. Ryne shook his head and settled one hand over Brimstone's, sliding it over his thigh and belly to settle over the bulge in his pants. The soldier chuckled softly.

"Good way to distract me from the pain," Ryne said, shifting to lean against one of Brimstone's arms instead of back against his chest.

"True," the soldier agreed before claiming another kiss and groping back. He shifted as well, pulling one knee up and bracing his foot on the cot behind Ryne, who sighed against his lips. Now Brimstone had the freedom to touch with both hands, and he shivered when the scientist took the same liberty.

"Touch me," the scientist asked quietly as his breaths sped up.

Closing his hand carefully against the apex of Ryne's thighs, Brimstone rubbed with the heel of his hand over the hard ridge. He sucked in a short breath as Ryne copied his movement, grasping below his belly.

After long moments of kissing and groping they both shuddered with arousal, and Brimstone unfastened their pants so hot hands could slide under the fabric. The soldier grunted as Ryne closed his fingers around his erection and pulled it free. Their touches were awkward as they moved just slightly, trying not to jar each other's injuries but wanting to find relief.

Ryne moaned as his cock was fisted, and he lifted his hips against it. "Good..." he moaned.

"Yeah," Brimstone agreed, dropping his lips to Ryne's collarbone. "Been too long — close, really close," he gasped.

"Yeah," Ryne echoed, and within another minute he grunted and stiffened as he came within Brimstone's fingers. The soldier wasn't far behind, biting his bottom lip as he jerked silently, his come shooting up to splatter on the warm skin under his torn-up shirt.

They held each other close, hot and sweaty, drowsing for a moment before Brimstone finally reached for a soft cloth in the First Aid kit to wipe up their mess. Then he settled back, pulling Ryne against him once again.

The scientist pressed his cheek against Brimstone's shoulder and shifted his hand up to coast over the now-unmarked belly and chest through the bloody ribbons of his tank. He paused over the tags. "What's this?" he asked, picking up the LCD chip attached to the same chain.

The V1 was quiet so long that Ryne shifted just enough to look up at him, and he saw heartfelt sorrow. "Brimstone... I'm sorry..."

Shaking his head, the soldier took the chip gently from Ryne's fingers and pushed the button on the top of it. A picture lit up brightly on the screen. It was him, standing with a blond man who held a small blonde girl. A little redheaded girl stood in front of them. They were all smiling, even the gruff soldier.

Ryne looked from the shining picture to the same shine reflecting in Brimstone's eyes. "Your family," he said.

Brimstone nodded. "I guess they're gone now," he murmured, his grief apparent. "Even if Evelyn and Laurie aren't... They were probably too young to remember me."

"I'm sure he made certain they knew you," Ryne said quietly, sliding an arm around the V1's back to hug him awkwardly. The soldier leaned his head against Ryne's, a tiny outward sign of emotional pain, while the scientist shifted too much and winced in physical pain. He settled more fully against Brimstone's chest, feeling very sleepy as the painkillers took effect.

"What will you do after this?" he asked. But he drifted off right after, leaving Brimstone to hold him close, eyes hooded.

"Nothing," Brimstone finally whispered. "But you will."


A few hours later, Brimstone stopped in front of Nighthawk near the door, dropping the heavy sack of explosives at their feet. They watched each other for a long moment, Nighthawk's dark eyes first reflecting stubbornness, then unhappiness, and finally resignation. Slowly he offered his hand.

The other V1 reached out to curl their palms together, hooking their thumbs, and their other hands covered the combined fist before they leaned in to press their foreheads together.

"You're in charge," Brimstone murmured. "No more leash."

"Always got to be the damn hero," Nighthawk murmured, his lips mere inches from Brimstone's. "I happen to like being on your leash."

"Fuck you, Liam," Brimstone answered fondly, mouth curving into an actual smile.

"Anytime, Malcolm, you know that," Nighthawk replied just as warmly. "Only I think you just might have your eye caught somewhere else."

Brimstone's hazel eyes closed for a long moment as they stood silently. "Take care of him," he said quietly to his friend. "And yourself."

"I will," Nighthawk agreed as they pulled apart slowly. Brimstone reached down to lift the bag and settled it on his shoulder as he picked up his gun. He got to the door, keyed it open, and turned to look back at Nighthawk from the threshold.

The other V1 watched him, arms folded, expressionless, and nodded ever so slightly. Nighthawk understood. Brimstone nodded in return and left.

RYNE ran through bright white halls, his feet thunking on the metal. Looking down at himself, he saw a V3 uniform, complete with heavy combat boots and a gun in his hands, but he wore a white lab coat over it all. Was he running toward something? Away from something? He ran through an endless maze of white. Then he turned a corner and ran right into a wall.

When he straightened back up, he noticed the wall was a man with pale skin and silver clothes and a dark shock of hair that curled about his ears, framing the face of a hawk. Huge silvered wings extended into the air behind him, flexed and spread, shining and smooth. Not at all like feathers. And when he looked at the man's eyes, he saw a glitter of black shine.

The walls fell away but the hawk remained as they stood atop a skyscraper, above a lit skyline that Ryne recognized, the stars above obscured by smog. As he focused on the familiar city, plumes of fire exploded, releasing belches of smoke and poison, the city burning and collapsing as he watched. A hand fell upon his shoulder and he looked up at the hawk that perched at his side.

"He is the Cleanser."

The world spun and he ran again, this time through the streets far below the buildings that reached to the stars, some ways below the cloudwalks where the normal people moved, eschewing the dirty realism of the Earth as it was now. They were the filth of humanity. Those left over and left behind as their genes pigeonholed them into slots of failure and forgetfulness. Every time he turned around, another faceless homeless figure reached out to him: some begging, some threatening. A loud explosion scared him, and he looked into the sky to see the rainbow of flames arching.

"He is the Destroyer."

Back in the facility now, the facility where he knew he worked, he stood in his lab, sedately mixing and splicing and crunching numbers with a computer's help, well away from the actual results. He held up the beaker and the clear solution turned to blood. Then the beaker shattered and the blood stained his hands as he screamed. A soft hand on his shoulder calmed him.

"He is the Deliverance."

It was Nighthawk, he realized distantly. The V1 floated beside him, an embodiment of his enhancements, sent by a criticized and shunned God who had waned since Man had become God in his own right. The path to the future was a narrow one, one that led to fewer and fewer members of humanity. He could see that now. He himself would fade into nothingness unless the progress of science was interrupted. But Nighthawk protected him as the lab burned down around them. How odd that it was he who stood here, a man with enhanced reflexes and strength. A soldier built for battle. But instead of fighting, he stood here, sheltering him. It should have been someone else.

Someone with the gift of healing, who could face any threat and survive. Someone whose focus on the protection of innocents was absolute.

"He is the Eternal."

He blinked to find himself in a gorgeous green garden, sitting at a patio table that held the remains of a pleasant lunch. He could hear the happy laughter of little girls, and two appeared out of nowhere running across the grass toward him, one with long red hair, holding the hand of a small toddling brunette.

"Papa, Papa, Daddy's gonna get us!" the older one called, and he felt himself grin as the other man appeared and swept the little girls up, one in each arm, turning them in a circle to garner more bubbling laughter. Daddy was smiling, bright and happy, reflecting joy and belonging as he looked over at Papa. Daddy's dark hair spilled over his brow to bracket glimmering hazel eyes, the scruff of his beard not obscuring the strong lines of his face. But as he continued to turn, laughing along with the little girls, he started to fade away like the sun burning off fog.

"No!" Papa yelled, the first sound he had forced from his throat, and he lurched from the chair to run toward his lover. The garden shimmered and disappeared, the laughter echoing into nothingness until all he could hear was his own harsh breathing as he ran.

The dichotomy was confusing, and so was the maze of white hallways and laboratories, the cryo morgues and computer centers, and he turned yet another corner to skid to a horrified stop. He staggered back and stared at the army of V3s that extended in front of him, back through the hall, no end to them in sight. But instead of touching him, hitting him, killing him, they filed past, an endless row on each side of him. He turned and caught his reflection in a mysteriously conjured window – no red hair. No beard, no distinctive nose, no lab coat. Only the cookie-cutter face of a V3 with dead, dull discs for eyes.

He screamed and turned to run, but he ran into something hot and hard and acrid, bouncing back and falling to the floor, hard. Transparent shadowed fingers of mist curled around the floor, wrapping up around his legs as he frantically scooted backward, trying to escape the oppressive heat that held him down. He looked up in terror at the blackened and smoking legs, leading up to an equally charred body to a face that bore grim, hooded eyes. Terror ripped through him as both hands raised over him, columns of flame and smoke rising above him.

"He is the Brimstone."

Ryne woke screaming.

"Ryne — *Ryne!*" Cary shook him until his screams died down and his terror calmed, and Nighthawk stood above them, watching him with concern. "Ryne, wake up. You're okay. We're okay."

"He's gone," the scientist gasped, wrapping his arms around himself. "He's gone, isn't he?"

Cary looked up at Nighthawk, who didn't say anything. "Ryne, how did you know that? You've been drugged and asleep for three hours."

"He's gone, I know it. He's gone to blow up the case, and he's not coming out of it," Ryne said shakily, sitting up.

After a tense moment, Nighthawk spoke. "What's your enhancement, Ryne?" But it sounded like he suspected.

The scientist shivered, looking first at Cary crouching at his knees, then up to the soldier. He could almost see the wings. "Foresight. Empathy. A sixth sense, of a sort," Ryne murmured.

"That's how you knew to suspect something. You picked up on it," Cary said. "Someone was thinking about it loud enough, with strong enough emotion, that you picked up on it." The engineer looked up at Nighthawk. "It's totally experimental. Not even designed until about six months ago." He looked back at Ryne with an accusation in his eyes. "You used yourself as a guinea pig."

"I already knew something was up. I thought the enhancement would be what I needed to figure out what was going on."

"All right, enough. We've got things to do to get out of here," Nighthawk said firmly. "How's your leg, Ryne?"

Shifting carefully, Ryne stood up with Cary's help and put weight on the injured limb. "Not bad, actually. Brimstone did a good job cleaning it up."

"Yeah," Nighthawk muttered as he walked over to his guns. "He's always been good at clean up."

Ryne blanched, and Cary touched his arm. "Ryne, there's no way you could have gone along with your leg. And it's safer, one man going into the case than four. Less chance of detection."

"He's not getting out," Ryne whispered.

"I know," Nighthawk said as he joined them again. "And he knows. Now suit up. Cary's got some computer magic to do."

They next stopped in a computer core just off the case, having negotiated the halls and even some ductwork to avoid V3 patrols. Cary clattered on the computer. "Ryne, I need the pass codes to get at the enhancement storage," he said.

The scientist joined him at the computer as he systematically wiped out all the current research, and the engineer sent out bugs and viruses to infect and corrupt database backups all over the country. Anything that had anything to do with the V3 project would be gone. He was looking through the files and with a jerk stopped the screen's movement, then jammed the comm pad into the port.

"What?" Ryne asked, frowning at Cary.

The other man transferred several chunks of data to the pad and then closed the connection, restarting the wipe. "That's all I can do from here," Cary said after several minutes, having ignored Ryne's inquiry. "Anything that's left will be pretty much useless once the nerve case is destroyed. But I have to get inside to start the viral sequence on the archive labs. Everything could be re-created with that information."

"We can't have that," Ryne said. "It has to end here."

Nighthawk studied the schematic Cary pulled up. "We go this way."

They had to fight their way in, and Nighthawk's strength and speed gave them an edge as the V3s didn't have time to sound an alarm. Cary got into a subcenter just within the case and plugged in the comm pad he'd programmed. "This is it," he murmured as he pressed the button to transfer the file.

Ryne watched as the bar crossed the pad, marking the copy process, and finally, *finally* it beeped and was done. Cary started typing as he opened the file and began the program, and the screen started to fuzz before code filled the screen. "It's working," the engineer said.

"We need to go," Nighthawk said sharply, grabbing them both by the sleeves and dragging them to the door.

"Wait!" Cary yelped, pulling free and running back to the console, where he grabbed the comm pad. He ran after Nighthawk and Ryne, right into a group of three V3s. One the V1 shot immediately, one he threw over his shoulder into the bulkhead, the other he had to grapple with. Cary and Ryne scooted out and ran down the hall, only to skid to a stop and run back toward the V1 as more implacable enemies turned the corner.

"Duck!" Nighthawk yelled, and they hit the floor as he sprayed bullets over them, taking out the V3s. He ran toward them and literally picked them up off the floor. "This way out," he said calmly, dragging Ryne along behind him as Cary hurried to keep up. The soldier had to let go as another group of V3s accosted them, and Cary joined him, jabbing sedatives into a V3's leg and dropping him like a log. Ryne stood back, breathing hard and gripping his own leg, when he heard something behind him. He turned to see dead eyes looking at him, and he was grabbed by the throat and lifted off his toes. Choking, Ryne beat at the hand while silver discs looked at him dispassionately.

Ryne heard a shot crack through the hallway and the V3 dropped him. He collapsed to the floor, barely scrambling out of the way as the huge body fell next to him. The scientist scooted back on his butt, looking up in shock to see Brimstone standing there, gun in hand and a tired smile on his face.

"Thought I told you to look out for him," the V1 said to Nighthawk, who picked Ryne up off the floor.

"Yeah, well, I was a little busy. 'Bout time you got here."

"Brimstone!" Cary exclaimed as he caught up.

"Brimstone," Ryne echoed. He got his balance, walked forward and kissed him hard. Brimstone didn't pull away at all; rather, one hand wrapped around Ryne's neck and held him there as they plundered each other's mouths. Nighthawk just grinned, sliding an arm about Cary and holding him close.

The V1 pulled back to look at the scientist. "You should always watch your back," he chastised, though gently.

"You're here to do it for me," Ryne said, smiling.

Brimstone huffed. "Come on. Let's get out of here."

Winding their way through the outer case complex, they were taken by surprise when a klaxon sounded and the lights went off, replaced by the deep, flashing red of emergency illumination. "Time to run," Brimstone urged.

They met another squad of V3s, and Nighthawk had a hard time of it, though Brimstone laid down a good spate of suppressive fire before abandoning the empty weapon. They managed to work their way through the melee, all drawing minor wounds before they broke free, making for the last hallway that led out.

Nighthawk led the way through the intersection, Cary and Ryne behind him, but Brimstone had to stop, fighting hand-to-hand with a V3 who barreled at them from the opposite hall. After a swift duck and sweep of a foot, the V1 dropped the enemy, stomped, and broke the soldier's sternum. Regaining his balance, Brimstone tried to dodge when he heard a bullet flying by, but another struck him in the side. He hit the opposite wall after making the corner but kept moving.

Nighthawk got through the door, which started to steadily close. "Shit, they're locking the case down," he hissed. "Brimstone – move it!" he called out into the dim hallway which had turned ruddy red.

The V1 further down the hall stretched his legs back into a run as Ryne and Cary hurried through the door. "C'mon!" Ryne urged.

Just as he turned the corner to catch up and still thirty yards away, Brimstone spun to the side and rammed into the wall as another couple bullets tore into him from behind. "No! Brimstone, c'mon!" Ryne yelled. The V1 struggled back up to run again, and Ryne choked as he realized the soldier wouldn't make it.

The door slid shut and locked just as Brimstone got there. He leaned against the door, breath rattling. "Go on, get outta here," he rasped through the small barred window just head-high. "Nighthawk. Twenty minutes," he said hoarsely as he raised dark, resigned eyes to Ryne's pained blue ones.

"Shit! No, I won't leave!" Ryne hissed as the V3s appeared from around the corner, striding toward Brimstone. "I *won't* leave you alone!" he insisted as he stuck his fingers through the bars.

The cold in Brimstone's gaze melted as he looked at Ryne, storing away the memory, and he raised one hand to knit their fingers together. "Ryne," he said quietly.

"No! I just found you..." Ryne said frantically, hitting the control pad with his other hand.

Brimstone heard the guns behind him being cocked. He reached behind his neck to snag the chain and pull his dog tags over his head. He pressed them into Ryne's hand and closed the redhead's palm over them.

"Brimstone," Ryne said, voice torn.

"It's Malcolm. M'name's Malcolm," the V1 said raggedly as the footsteps stopped twenty feet away. "Now go. Please."

"Malcolm..." Ryne objected as Cary and Nighthawk grabbed his arms to pull him away. "No! No, Malcolm!"

Brimstone watched him for a moment, overcome with regret, but reassured by the tags swinging in Ryne's grasp. Then he straightened his shoulders and turned around.

Ryne screamed again as he heard the rattle of muffled gunfire striking the door, but Nighthawk was dragging him away, and it was too dark for him to see. The scientist kicked and struggled against the V1's incredible strength until Nighthawk slammed him back against a wall. "Pull it together! Don't make it mean any less," he growled. Ryne sagged and Cary took his hand to pull him along as they again started running down the hall, away from the case.

Away from Brimstone.


EMPLOYEES running pell mell for the exits clogged the hallways of the main scientific complex, some with comm pads, others with boxes of research, trying to clear the building after the evacuation and lockdown announcement. The red lights still illuminated the hallways, making every motion seem that much more sinister. Cary ducked into a lab and snatched three white jackets from a closet, and just like that the three men blended in with the crowd.

"I need to stop at my office," Cary insisted. "I need that research or we'll lose everything we've worked on that's good."

Nighthawk stopped with them in the hallway as scientists pushed past them carelessly. The V1 didn't look at all happy. "We've got about twelve minutes to get out of here," he hissed.

"Two minutes, that's all I need," Cary promised, darting around the corner. The soldier glanced at his watch unhappily and turned his chin see Ryne leaning against the wall in the corner, away from the foot traffic. He was staring at the floor.

"Hey, Ryne, is there anything you want to take with you?" Nighthawk asked as he walked over out of the busy hallway. When Ryne flinched, the V1 realized what he'd said. "Ryne, you gotta understand. This is what we signed up for. He knew that."

"You didn't sign up for this. He didn't sign up for this — having to take out the government and system that created you," Ryne growled, hands curled into fists. "It's a goddamn revolution and he won't be here to see it."

"But he made it happen," Nighthawk said quietly. "That's what's important. That he did what was right. That was Brimstone. Not just following orders."

Ryne sighed and laid his head back, lifting his hand and looking at the tags he still clutched. "I just met him. Why do I feel this strongly about him?"

Nighthawk grinned. "Part of our irresistible charm, I'd expect."

Snorting, Ryne curled the chain around his hand. "You're charming. Malcolm was gruff under the best of circumstances."

"Nah, you just didn't see him away from the job. Sometimes he'd even smile on off nights," Nighthawk confided.

Ryne smiled, chuckling a little. "You'll have to tell me more about him sometime."

"You're on," Nighthawk said. The V1 stepped close and took the tags out of Ryne's hand, straightened the chain and dropped it over the scientist's head so the tags hung to the middle of his chest. "He deserves to be remembered."

"Yeah," Ryne said, looking over Nighthawk's shoulder as Cary ran back toward them, pushing through the crowd.

"Let's go," Nighthawk said, taking both of them by the arm. "Just under nine minutes. Where do we get out?"

"The train tubes are that way, single vehicles that way," Cary pointed.

"Can you steal a car like in the good old days?" Nighthawk asked.

Ryne raised an eyebrow. "Ah... No?"

Nighthawk frowned. "We'll chance it. We should be able to find a way out regardless."

Cary led the way as they ran, pushing through other employees on their quest for freedom and safety. In some ways, Ryne wanted to say something to some of them. *Run, get out, it's not just chaos, it's not just a lockdown. If you don't leave, you're going to die.* But there just wasn't time... and he wasn't feeling particularly compassionate.

With Nighthawk's strength, breaking into the garage was simple, and the V1 surprised them with enough mechanical skill to get the garage doors open while Cary overrode the vehicle's drive codes. As they climbed into the shuttle car, more people streamed into the large room.

"Damn, people are going nuts," Nighthawk muttered.

"We've never had an emergency like this. Who would set the alarms off?" Cary asked.

"They must have found the explosives," Ryne said.

"No. Brimstone did it," Nighthawk said, voice sure.

"What? Why?" Cary asked.

"To get as many civilians out as possible. The V3s won't leave, but the scientists and engineers and everyone else will at least try to get out," Nighthawk explained. "And, by the way, great evac procedures you got here," the V1 muttered, settling in the front passenger seat.

"We don't have any 'evac procedures'," Cary exclaimed from the pilot's position. "It's supposed to be a secure facility. Why would it ever need to be evacuated?"

"Would you two shut up?" Ryne said, smacking Cary in the arm after buckling himself in near the back glass. "Get us out of here."

Cary got the shuttle going and it shot out the doors, following the track laid for it that led under and out of the complex. Nighthawk looked at his watch. "Can this thing go any faster?"

The engineer pushed some buttons, trying to get the shuttle more speed. "We've maxed out," he said as the concrete walls flashed by.

"This is gonna be close," Ryne murmured, voice turned melancholy. If he'd had a choice about where to die — he'd have rather died with Malcolm. So Malcolm wouldn't have had to be alone.

"One minute," Nighthawk said. Cary entered more codes into the computer, kicking at the console when it bleeped at him and turned red. The engineer reached down between his legs, pulled open a small panel, reached in and yanked out some wiring. The console flickered and turned green.

"Thirty seconds," the V1 said steadily as Cary pushed another series of buttons, and the shuttle accelerated noticeably, shooting through the curves of the tunnel like some sort of roller coaster.

"There's the opening," Cary pointed out as they rounded a curve and saw a halo of hazy light.

"Fifteen seconds." Nighthawk's voice was strained as the shuttle car shot out of the complex and into the large lot, moving toward the outer fences.

Ryne turned around and looked out the back, raising one hand to press his palm to the glass. He held Malcolm's tags tight in his other hand.

"Five. Four. Three. Two. One."

Nothing.

"My watch could be a little off," Nighthawk murmured, glancing over his shoulder.

Nothing.

"Oh God," Ryne whispered, face going white. "We have to go back. We can't let them keep building V3s."

"Go back? We can't go back!" Cary insisted, though he slowed the shuttle as it neared the far gate. "We'd be shot on sight!"

Nothing.

Nighthawk stared at his watch, lips compressed.

"We can't just give up, Cary. They're destroying the meaning of everything we've ever done! They'll take over the country and start murdering people wholesale!" Ryne exclaimed.

"They'll murder us!" Cary objected.

"They already murdered Malcolm! We have to do something!"

The core of the building exploded.

It sent out a shockwave that knocked the car off the track and sent it skidding to land against the concrete wall that extended around the perimeter of the concrete lot. The plume of flame and smoke from the center of the complex flew into the clouds, sending a flash of light and a wall of heat out from the facility in a lapping wave.

Shocked, Ryne watched out the side window. He was dazed, horrified, and a tiny bit thankful. But it didn't banish the tears from his eyes. Cary reached back to squeeze his shoulder, and Ryne limply covered Cary's hand with his own, patting it in a motion of gratitude. Nighthawk was watching, too, his face a frozen mask. It didn't hide the sorrow in his brown eyes.

Grasping for the door, Ryne opened the shuttle and climbed out shakily, looking back at the burning building. People were still running out. Most of the outer facility would probably survive more or less intact, unless the fire spread. As long minutes crawled past, he became aware of the other two men standing next to him silently, but still he watched the fire. It hurt. It felt like mourning.

*Beep-beep. Beep-beep. Beep-beep.*

Nighthawk glanced down at his watch, stared at it for a moment, and then shut off the alarm. "Guys, stay here, okay?" he said.

"Stay here? What? Why?" Cary asked, grasping Nighthawk's arm.

"The whole place didn't blow. There's some things we need if we're going to start over, right? I can salvage enough to set us up real well," the V1 said, slinging the gun over his shoulder. "There's profit in chaos. You two stay together. I'll be back soon." With no more explanation than that, he was off, impossibly fast as he ran across the concrete back to the tunnel and into the complex.

"Now what?" Cary asked tiredly.

"I don't know. Everything's changed," Ryne murmured. "Everything. The military's gone. The government will follow once the people figure out what's happening and totally freak. I don't think the local authorities will be able to do anything."

Cary nodded. "It's going to be a huge mess for a long time."

"Yeah. I planned for it, but I never really expected to see it happen," Ryne said.

"Planned for it?" Cary asked, frowning. "What're you talking about?"

"I bought my own scientific facility, out in the metroplex, away from the inner city. It's pretty much set up so I can continue my research there and set up a clinic to start doing enhancements free of charge."

"How are you going to do that? All enhancements have to be paid for, there's the governmental... fees..." Cary's voice trailed off. If there was no government, there would be no fees. No rules. No restrictions.

Ryne smiled wryly. "If we don't want this to happen again, the genetic enhancements have to be available to everyone. The government has to be protecting us, not squeezing us for every dime, every resource. We have to invest in the future or we won't have one," Ryne explained. "That was the other vision I had. If enhancements kept narrowing and specializing people, soon the country would be so inbred that the population would die off."

Cary slid down to sit with his back against the car. "Everything's going to be different."

"Yeah. Everything," Ryne echoed as he sat next to him. They watched the facility burn. It was a grim sort of Independence Day.

Ryne woke up to see Cary pacing back and forth in front of him. The scientist glanced at his watch. Three hours. "Cary?"

"He's not back yet. How long could it take? What's he getting? Why's it taking so long?"

Ryne woke up fully, eyes widening, and he caught Cary's hand and tugged lightly. "Sit down here. We have no idea how long it will take." He looked toward the complex. The flames weren't nearly as high now, but the dark, heavy smoke had dropped to the ground, obscuring the view as the wind blew it this way and that. "So you think we can get the shuttle back on the track?"

"No way. But Nighthawk could," Cary said, settling back down next to the scientist. "Way too heavy for us."

Looking over at his friend, Ryne leaned his head back against the shuttle. "You like him."

Cary sighed, turning his light blue eyes to Ryne. "Yeah," he said, though it sounded hollow. "I mean, we kinda clicked, you know? Sure, the sex was great and really helped with the nerves. Which was probably the point," he said wryly. "But also... we clicked. You know?"

Ryne's eyes were faraway. "Yeah," he echoed. "I know."

"Was it like that for you?" Cary asked quietly.

"No. Not at first. Not even later. We didn't match, didn't have equal footing, didn't get along. And then it all changed. I'm not sure why. I'm guessing he changed, because I'm pretty sure I didn't. As to why he did..." Ryne shrugged. His face transformed with grief, and one hand slid under the lab coat to grasp the tags that hung from his neck. "I could have loved him."

Cary didn't answer, he just lifted one hand and squeezed Ryne's shoulder. The redhead sighed and stared out into the shifting smoke. After awhile, between wisps, he thought he saw something moving. He squinted, leaning back and forth, and the smoke cleared again, just enough. "He's back," Ryne said, standing up. He'd caught a glimpse of Nighthawk moving in their direction at a slow walk.

Cary tried to see him, obviously fretting. "What's taking so long? He can move faster than this."

"He's carrying something, whatever he went to get. If it's heavy, I'm sure it's slowing him down," Ryne placated.

But the engineer wouldn't wait. He dashed off into the smoke toward Nighthawk, and Ryne clambered up to follow the man's flapping lab coat. When he straightened, he stopped in place, watching them emerge from the smoke.

Nighthawk walked with Cary under one arm – and Brimstone supported by the other.

Ryne swallowed hard. "Oh God..." he whispered. "Malcolm." And then he was running toward them.

Brimstone looked up with an exhausted smile when he saw Ryne approaching. He pulled away from Nighthawk, favoring one leg, and caught Ryne up against him. They would have toppled backward to the ground if Nighthawk hadn't held Brimstone up until he had his balance again. The V1's eyes closed as he wrapped his arms around Ryne snugly, dropping his head to press his lips lightly to his temple. The scientist hugged him tight, promising himself he'd never let go. He didn't know how Brimstone was here – how he survived, how he got out, how Nighthawk knew how to find him – too many questions. They could be answered later. For now, Ryne just held Brimstone tight.

"Well, despite it being nearly the end of the world as we know it, I'm thinking this is a happy ending," Nighthawk said with a grin as he wrapped his arm around Cary's neck while the engineer laughed and nodded.

"I'll agree with that," Brimstone rasped, looking down at the scientist with tired but shining eyes.

Ryne shifted to look up at him and raised a hand to wipe a trickle of blood away from the corner of Malcolm's mouth. "No... I think it's a happy beginning."

# CLOSE ENCOUNTER

...BEEP. Beep. Beep. Beep...

A dark-headed man under the blankets shifted, turned in the messy bunk, and threw his arm over his eyes, annoyed by the mechanical sound disturbing his sleep.

...Beep. Beep. BEEP. BEEP...

With an aggrieved sigh, Tris rolled to his back and cracked open an eye, peering through stringy, matted hair across the dimmed cabin at the control panel where several red lights blinked.

He jerked so hard when the cabin door banged open that he almost fell out of the bunk.

"Wake up, Tris, we're on approach and you're hung over, you bastard." Mill swore as he grabbed for the control panel, punching buttons and interrupting the beeping.

A rumpled Tris blinked owlishly at Mill and then yelped as the ship lurched to the side once Mill took control of the helm.

"We dropped out of hyper right into a debris field," Mill reported as the blast shield opened, revealing star-studded space dotted with jagged hunks of metal in front of the ship.

Tris shook his head, trying to clear it, only to slide off his bunk as Mill cursed and steered the ship hard to port to avoid a piece of tumbling debris.

Picking himself up off the floor, Tris stumbled as the ship veered around the clumps of broken pods. He clung to the back of Mill's seat as the craft swerved.

"Starboard, starboard!" Tris yelled as several pieces of flotsam threatened them. "Thirty degrees down angle, veer to starboard..." Tris said as Mill gripped the controls.

"I've got it, I've got it," Mill growled.

"Shit, what the hell happened here?" Tris asked under his breath as he studied the mess out in space.

"Where the hell am I supposed to be going?" Mill asked. He leaned over the navigation panel, sweating.

Tris leaned over to the terminal. "260 X-axis."

"Tris..."

"By 75 Y-axis."

"Tris!"

"Positive Z-axis for three minutes – that's the carrier."

"*Goddamnit* Tris, get over here before we get smeared!" Mill yelled.

Tris's head snapped around to see the mess hurtling toward their ship from all directions. He grabbed for the controls and pushed Mill out of the pilot's chair.

Mill fell to his knees and skidded across the decking as Tris threw the ship into a downward spiral, jerking the craft around space junk and turning toward the nearby carrier at the same time.

Pieces of scrap metal skimmed over the ship and smaller pieces clanked off a side panel before Tris steered them clear of the debris field.

"Fucking hell." Mill sat on the deck and let his head sag back against the bulkhead.

Tris keyed the radio and contacted the carrier, receiving clearance to dock. Once his ship was secure in the tractor beam, he turned to Mill with a toothy smile.

"We're here already? Hell, that was fast," he quipped, looking down at his friend.

Mill muttered under his breath and wiped a trail of sweat from soaked blonde hair at his temple. "Good thing I happened to hear the proximity alarm when we came out of hyper."

"You did great, Mill. You've learned a hell of a lot about piloting in the last year," Tris said, voice full of praise.

Mill sighed and looked pointedly at Tris. "Good thing the ace was here to bail our asses out."

Tris groaned and held his head. "The ace is hung over."

Mill snorted and glanced back at his stubbled captain. "You've been drunk for three days, Tris."

He rubbed at his face, pushing back the limp hair from his face. He pulled at his shirt and sniffed. "Three days? Fuck me. That was *some* liquor, then."

Mill rolled his eyes. "We're in the clear. You've got time to get cleaned up."

Tris made a dismissive grunt. "They're just medic pukes. All they need to do is pay me. I don't put on airs for anyone."

"Did you take a look at the cargo?" Mill asked.

"Nah. I just had them load it up and lock it down," Tris said as he stretched.

Mill looked back at him. "We're getting good money for this, right?"

"The best," Tris drawled, closing his eyes again.

Mill sighed. "I hope so. I hate having live cargo on my hands."

Tris didn't even twitch. "Who cares if it's live? Not like it's mobile."

"Too many years in the service."

Tris opened an eye and peered at Mill's tidy jumpsuit and clean-shaven face. "Yeah. You don't quite fit the privateer's image, Mill."

Mill stood and patted the captain's leg before he walked out of the cabin. "You've enough image for both of us, Tris."

TRIS lounged outside the hatch, now grudgingly reattired in dusty boots, worn leather and loose cotton. He punched a couple buttons on the hand remote and the ship's cargo bay door opened.

Mill walked out of the ship, heading toward the docking bay door, two stacks of long, metal cylinders strapped to a motorized tug trundling along behind him.

"Tris, I see you haven't changed."

The captain looked up to see a tall man in a black military jumpsuit enter the docking bay. Tris grinned and stood to meet him. "Rey. Great to see you, man."

Rey accepted Tris's offer to clasp arms. "Thanks for bringing the cargo on such short notice," he said.

Tris shrugged. "Money talks. And for this trip, it screamed."

Mill glanced at them as he walked by, the tug following. He stopped to listen and the secured cylinders shuddered as the tug halted as well. He looked over the newcomer, silently approving of the close-cropped haircut and closely trimmed goatee. It fit with the man's military demeanor.

"It's important that the research here continue uninterrupted," Rey said, walking over to check the small, computerized displays on the cylinders.

Mill perked up. "Research?"

"Rey, this is Mill. Mill, Rey. And Rey's business is not our business, Mill. We deliver the cargo, we get paid, and we leave," the captain said dismissively.

Rey blinked at the console, then turned his chin sharply toward his friend. "They didn't tell you what you were transporting?"

Mill shook his head, looking grim. "Told you we should have asked, Tris," he muttered.

Rey gestured to the cylinder on top. "These patients are highly critical cases. They may give us the final breakthrough to beat 728PM."

Tris went totally still. "What?"

"You mean... They're..." Mill's eyes widened and he looked at the cylinders in shock.

"Blue Stripes?" Tris interrupted in a strained whisper. "We were transporting Blue Stripes and they didn't even tell us?"

Rey nodded slowly and swallowed, shrugging.

They all turned to look at the cylinder Rey had touched. It had spun in place to expose a clear view port. The patient hung suspended inside, frozen in place by cryotechnology.

"Yeah. Blue Stripes," Rey confirmed. "We've about got it beat. The docs think these patients may have the final answer to beating the virus."

Mill was pale and his jaw tightened grimly. "All right. Nothing to be done for it now. Let's get these ... people ... inside. Where they need to be."

The captain stared at the patient in the top cylinder – he was a young man. Dark brown waves surrounded what was in life probably a very pretty face: triangular, shaped by sharp cheekbones, a tapered chin, and thin pink lips. The closed eyes tilted up at the corners, like he was of Oriental extraction. But right now the face was pale and drawn, like wax.

Rey nodded, and he was reaching for the tug's controls when an alarm blared. Before anyone could react, the carrier lurched violently, throwing the men across the docking bay. Tris slid right into the tug and its cylinders while Rey and Mill fell in different directions. They climbed to their feet, only to fall again as the ship lurched and a call to stations sounded.

"Fuck – they found us," Rey yelled. "You guys got to get outta here and get clear."

"They? Who're they?" Mill yelled.

Tris stared at the face in the cylinder while he held onto it to keep from getting thrown. He suddenly knew who was attacking. He turned to Rey, who had regained his balance. "It's a Bluumeaan attack squad. That was what the debris was outside – scout ships."

The look on Rey's face confirmed Tris's answer. "We thought we'd gotten them before they transmitted our position. Looks like we were wrong," the soldier said. "These people have to be secured. Let's get them to Medical." Mill nodded and soon they moved into the carrier proper, the tug of cylinders following.

When the three men stumbled into the medical bay, the tug got stuck in the door as another internal explosion shook the carrier. Doctors and technicians rushed about the chaotic lab.

"Are you sure this is where we should take them?" Mill asked, peering into the dark, hazy laboratory. He bumped against the wall as a couple technicians pushed past him carrying stacks of data cards.

"This is where the containment section is. Nowhere else to go," Rey explained. "Let's get them inside."

The three men moved some debris and got the tug into the lab, and the mechanical door finally slid shut.

"Just how much shit are we in here, Rey?" Tris asked.

Rey moved to a desktop display and punched some buttons. He started talking to someone elsewhere on the ship, requesting a status report.

A broken and harried voice answered. "... carrier is taking heavy damage ... fighters are almost wiped out ... attack squad has boarded ... don't know how to stop them – can't get away ... bridge gone ... officers gone. Abandon ship!"

Rey growled in frustration. "That's it then. We'll have to save the research and the doctors and get the hell out of here." He stalked over to a cabinet on the wall and hit an access code to pop the seal. The doors slid open to reveal a stash of powered rifles.

Mill glanced over to the cylinders. "What about them?"

Tris followed Mill's gaze, trying to get the patient's pale face out of his head. He almost missed catching the rifle Rey tossed to him.

"I'll take one with me. The rest will have to be left behind," Rey answered, slinging a blaster over his shoulder.

Tris cut to the chase. "So you'll leave them here to die?"

"They're already dead," Rey said harshly. "They're critical cases with zero chance of recovery. They're technically alive only because they were put on ice for transport. Otherwise they'd be dead already."

"Then why take one?" Mill asked. He accepted a rifle, holding it awkwardly.

Rey jabbed a finger at the cylinders. "These patients hold the key to beating 728PM. Without one of them all the research and work is useless. If all four die – so does humanity."

The last words echoed in the lab just as a stronger explosion shook the science vessel. Several ceiling panels crashed to the floor with a huge puff of smoke and hissing steam poured into the lab.

"Go on, you've got to get moving." Rey shook his head at the mess, trying to climb over it to get to a computer station.

Tris stared at the cylinders until Mill pulled on his arm. "C'mon Tris, there's nothing we can do."

"The doctors are in the escape vessel; it'll jettison any time. You need to get back to your ship," Rey said.

Tris looked to him. "What about you?"

Rey glanced around the lab. "I have to make sure there's nothing here the Blue Meanies can use against us. Then I'll blow the rest of the carrier."

"With you on it?" Mill's voice peaked in disbelief.

"I sure as hell hope not," Rey barked. "There's another escape pod. I'll just have to set it on auto and wait for someone to pick me up."

"And if the Blue Meanies pick you up?" Tris asked from his place in the doorway.

"Get out of here!" Rey waved them off and started punching keys, working at wiping the computers as the other two fled.

Mill and Tris stumbled through the abandoned white corridors as the carrier shook. Using indented hatches as grab handles, they pulled themselves along the passageways as fast as they could run. Incoming fire noisily struck the hull and broke through; more alarms rang out and air hissed dangerously as they approached the docking bay door.

Mill hit the access panel. It flared red and wouldn't open. Tris kicked the wall panel open and started messing with the wires while Mill frowned and looked at the hatch seals.

"Tris..."

"Gimme a sec, Mill, it's been awhile since I hotwired anything," Tris muttered.

"Tris, stop!" Mill reached down and jerked Tris away from the panel.

"What the fuck?" Tris stared at Mill, who pointed at the heavy metal door.

Ice crystals were forming on the seam as the tiniest bit of air seeped from their side to vacuum.

"*Oh fuck*," Tris whispered.

"C'mon, back to Rey ... away from here ..." Mill hurriedly pulled Tris to his feet, and they ran back down the corridor, rifles jerking on their shoulders. They tried to run faster when a startling crack deafened them and they heard the metal of the door give way to the ice cold of space.

They both felt the pull of air sucking them backward while struggling for the hatch at the end of the hallway. It was closing, but they made it through just before the emergency bulkhead sealed – the metal doors trapped Tris's pants leg and he had to rip it free.

Mill slid down the wall on the other side of the interior bulkhead, trying to catch his breath. "That ... was too ... close ..." he gasped.

Pulling his torn pants leg together, Tris frowned. "What about my ship?" he rasped.

"Either floating in one piece ... or in pieces. C'mon, only one way to find out." Mill climbed to his feet and pulled on the captain's arm.

They started threading their way back to Medical, detouring around another hull breach and helping some people out of a room where the door was jammed half-shut because part of the decking had caved in. The carrier was breaking apart around them noisily.

They had to climb through another fallen wall when they reached Medical. Tris yelled over the alarms, "Rey! Rey!"

They searched the wrecked lab and found the other man under a broken steel beam. Luckily, it was braced on the terminal above him.

Mill pulled Rey out from under the desk. The soldier groaned, reaching for his head, hand coming away bloody. "What hit me?" he asked dazedly.

Tris chuckled. "The ceiling. You're lucky you're not pulp."

Rey sighed and pointed to a medikit. "Get me that, will you?"

Mill picked his way around the lab as Tris wrapped up the shallow but messy head wound. They all winced each time another explosion echoed through the massive vessel.

"You get done?" Tris asked Rey as he repacked the medikit and then hooked it to his belt.

Rey nodded, patting his breast pocket. "Yeah, got what I need here. The rest is wiped. Why did you come back?" he asked.

"Bay got blown. Nowhere else to go but back here," Tris answered.

Rey nodded. "There's room for four in the pod. You can pilot the thing."

Another explosion, this one deep and violent, rocked the deck beneath them. Rey blanched. "We need to get a cylinder and get moving. That was the engine core."

He reached across the terminal and cut off the klaxon, plunging the room into sudden silence. Tris stood, looking for his shipmate. "Mill! We've got trouble!"

Mill's head popped up from across the room. "You don't know the half of it, guys."

Rey and Tris crossed the lab to what was left of the containment ward – it was blown wide open. The cylinders lay scattered, two of them smashed under bulkheads, one still intact but burnt, melted and black inside. Mill knelt on the floor next to the last one.

Tris swallowed hard as Rey cursed. The cylinder had been struck at the foot, popping off the hatch and breaking the seal. The patient was gone.

TRIS and Mill jogged behind Rey as they wound through the carrier. They'd stared at the empty cylinder for a full minute before another violent outburst had prodded them out of their shock.

Now they were fleeing for their lives.

Rey turned to look back at them as he stopped at a cross corridor. "I need to stop in here and get a few things. You guys okay?" Tris waved a hand, and Rey nodded. The soldier pointed to another hatch. "That's a small galley. See if there's anything useful we can take."

Tris followed Mill into the galley where they started rifling the cabinets.

"Tris, do you believe what Rey said about the patients and the Blue Stripes? That those patients were our last hope?" Mill asked.

Tris glanced up. "I believe him," he said quietly.

"And those cylinders that busted open – are we exposed? Is it an airborne transmission? I know it's really virulent but not much more than that," Mill rattled off. "I don't mind admitting I'm scared witless."

"You're not exposed."

Mill and Tris turned to gape at the slight, white-covered figure standing in the doorway.

"728PM is transmitted by skin and fluid contact. It cannot survive more than ten seconds on inanimate objects or in open air," the young man said, his voice sure. "The Bluumeaans designed it that way."

Tris swallowed, taking in the man who almost blended into the white metal walls. The captain couldn't drag his eyes away from the delicate features of his face. "You're the patient."

The young man nodded, his blue-tinged face solemn.

"So... we can't get it unless we touch you." Mill said.

"Unless you touch my skin with your skin," the young man clarified. "Fabric contact is safe." He held up his arms. The white bodysuit covered every bit of him from foot to fingertip, even up his neck where it fastened tightly under his chin. Only his head was exposed, with brown hair curling down past his shoulders.

Tris shuffled a bit. "You weren't in the cylinder."

The young man shook his head. "I rolled out. Took me several minutes to get my head back on straight."

Mill frowned. "Aren't you dying?" He stiffened when he realized how rude his words were.

The young man stilled, Tris noticed. Before that, some part of the patient had always been in motion – a hand moving, a foot tapping, a hip swaying. A side effect of the cold storage?

"That doesn't mean we leave him behind," Rey said from the doorway. The patient turned to look at the soldier, surprised. Tris raised an eyebrow as well.

"What's going on anyway? We're under attack?" the patient asked as Tris and Mill loaded a carryall Rey had thrown to them with food packs.

Rey nodded. "Bluumeaans. We've got to get you off this carrier and back to the doctors."

Mill seemed a little edgy as he approached the patient, but he tried not to flinch. The young man stepped back so Mill could pass. "Yes, I understand." The young man smiled for the first time and Tris was shell-shocked as a line of fire flashed through him. "I know I'm going to die, but I'd rather not be alone for it."

Rey nodded and glanced at his watch. "We're running out of time. Let's move." He pulled on Mill's arm and they moved down the corridor, leaving Tris and the patient to follow.

"I'm Tris. What's your name?" the captain asked as they started to run.

"Retter."


THE four men rushed headlong through the corridors of the dying carrier, Rey at point. Finally he stopped and cursed, smashing his fist into an already broken display at the closed bulkhead door in front of him.

"What? What's wrong?" Mill asked as Tris and Retter caught up, both out of breath.

"The bulkhead's fused. We're going to have to go around, but that means going down several sections. *Fuck*!" Rey banged his head back against the wall in frustration.

"So? We go down, then we come back up, right?" Tris said.

"Down toward the engine compartments, down toward more bays open to vacuum, and down toward the Blue Meanies," Rey said.

Retter's eyes flickered between the men while he watched from several steps away. He shifted from foot to foot, knowing he had nothing to contribute to help.

Mill sighed. "We go or we die here, right?"

Rey took a breath, closed his eyes and nodded. "Yeah. We go."

They all followed Rey around a corner, backtracking until he stopped at a door and keyed some buttons. The hatch slid open to reveal a vertical access tube with a ladder inside.

"I figure this is safer than going through the labs. We're so close to the outer hull here, some of them are sure to be open to space," Rey said, slinging a satchel and a rifle over his torso.

Mill and Tris peered down the tube. It was big enough for two of them to squeeze inside, were there a floor. Not a lot of room, just an access area for maintenance.

A distant whine caught their attention. Rey frowned as he cocked his head to listen. "They're moving this way. Let's move. I'm first, then Mill, then the patient, then Tris."

"Retter. His name is Retter," Tris said. The young man looked at him with huge brown eyes, surprised.

Rey glanced between the two. "Tea and crumpets later, okay? Let's go." He swung into the tube and started climbing down the ladder.

Mill watched him go, a frown heavy on his face. But he followed without a word, the carryall of food packs over his shoulder, the strap twisted against the rifle slung beside it.

Retter stepped forward and looked down. When he lifted his hand to grasp the ladder, it was shaking. He actually jerked when Tris laid a hand on his shoulder.

"Hey, you okay?" Tris asked quietly.

Retter stared at him in silent wonder. Tris blinked. "What?" he asked.

Retter glanced at Tris's hand.

Tris pulled it away slowly. "Sorry, I didn't think..." he started.

"No, it's fine," Retter interrupted. "It's just that no one touches, you know, because of..." he shrugged.

Tris's face rearranged from an annoyed scrunch to a determined set. He replaced his hand on Retter's shoulder and squeezed briefly. "Go on. I'll be right behind – uh – above you."

Retter smiled and stepped onto the ladder, climbing down.

MILL'S breathing echoed loudly in his ears. He felt like he'd been climbing down the ladder forever. "How we doing, Rey?" he called down.

Rey's voice filtered up to him. "Only two more levels, then we're out of here."

"Thank God," Mill muttered. "You hear that, Tris?" he pitched his voice up. He could see Retter several feet above him. "We're almost there."

Tris's voice filtered down. "I'm about ready for those crumpets, myself."

Mill laughed, and he heard laughter from the other men echoing around him as well.

After several more minutes, Mill heaved a sigh of relief when Rey hooted in success and light flooded the tube from a newly opened hatch.

Rey levered himself out and set his satchel and rifle on the floor, waiting as Mill's legs came into view.

Mill whistled a little tune as he approached the light. Just as he was stepping out onto the deck another heavy explosion rocked the carrier and he lost his balance, falling backward with a surprised yell.

Rey darted forward and grabbed the front of Mill's jumpsuit, yanking the other man toward him and out of the access tube. They fell backward, sprawling across one another and sliding across the deck as the carrier pitched.

The power flickered as sparks flew, drawing curses from Rey who rolled to his hands and knees and crawled back to the access tube. The door was mostly blocked, frozen in place. There was no way anyone would fit through the hole.

"Tris? Retter?" Rey called through the hole. Colorful cursing from Tris and a faint "I'm here" were his answers. The soldier sagged, relieved.

After a nervous wait, white-clad legs came into view and kept climbing down. Retter paused to look at the frozen door, his lips compressing a bit. Even with his slight build, he wouldn't fit. He shook his head and climbed down further so Tris could descend and talk to Rey.

Tris's face showed his supreme annoyance as Mill joined Rey at the blocked hatch. "This is perfect, Rey. Now what?" Tris asked, frustration clear in his voice. He glanced down the tube to see Retter's face peering up at him.

"You're going to have to go down two more levels, all right? Go down two, then get out of the maintenance tube. There's another access point about a thousand yards down that corridor to our left." Rey pointed. "Then get in that tube and come back up to this level. We'll meet you there."

Tris sighed. "Lovely. A thousand yards. Fuck you for working on a goddamn monster carrier, Rey. Save some crumpets for me and Retter, all right?"

"Take care, Tris," Mill murmured as the captain's head disappeared out of sight.

Rey tugged at Mill's arm. "C'mon, let's go find a secure room down by the next tube. As Tris implied, we'll have time to eat."

Mill nodded and followed Rey through the darkened corridor. After several minutes of stumbling through the black, Rey led him into a section with power. Mill sighed in relief, relaxing a little now that he could see around him.

Rey walked like a man with a purpose. There were more long empty passageways, one after another. After passing through the third hatchway, he pointed. "That's the access tube." He glanced around and walked over to key open a door. "C'mon, let's rest a bit."

Mill followed Rey into a nicely appointed lounge with some tables and several chairs, a couple of computer terminals and a long couch along the back wall. It even had carpet, which struck Mill as bizarre. He moved to collapse on the couch as Rey poked at a terminal, muttering under his breath.

"What is it?" Mill asked.

"Most everything is offline," Rey waved his hand in the air. "Go figure."

"Can you get any useful information?" Mill asked, stretching a bit.

Rey frowned and typed at the terminal some more, harrumphing as it just buzzed at him. "No. No interior cameras or life signs, no life support status, no communications."

Rey thumped the computer for good measure and collapsed into a chair. He dropped his rifle and satchel and reached for the bag of food packs. Mill watched him pull a couple out and read the tags.

"You really going to eat that?" Mill asked.

Rey shrugged. "I'm hungry. It's food."

"Meals Rejected by Ethiopians," Mill said with a chuckle.

"Ethi-who?" Rey asked, confused.

Mill shook his head. "Old, old joke. Really old. Refers to starving Africans."

"Africans?" Rey asked, still confused, as he pulled a pocketknife out and opened the package.

"You're not from Earth?" Mill asked, a little surprised.

Rey shook his head. "Company family. Born in the Zealand Clean Colonies. I've never been to Earth."

Mill raised an eyebrow. "Doctors, yeah?"

Rey nodded, tossing an open package to Mill. "And scientists, yeah. Yourself?"

"Born on Earth, European Megloplex. I've been to the colonies, though. I was in the service."

"It shows."

Mill cocked an eyebrow.

Rey chuckled, pointing at Mill's jumpsuit and waving at his clean-cut hairstyle, similar to his own close-cropped head. "You don't exactly have the privateer image going on."

Mill rolled his eyes.

They ate the food packs quickly, Rey keeping an ear out for any sounds that might be coming from down the corridor.

Mill stood up and moved to the door. "So, how do we know whether what we hear coming is Tris and Retter... or the Blue Meanies?"

When Rey didn't answer, Mill glanced back at him. "Rey?"

The soldier just looked at him evenly. "We don't," he finally answered quietly.

Mill frowned and stared back down the corridor. Rey's face folded in thought. "What did you do in the service, Mill? You don't act like you know much about fighting."

Mill shook his head. "I was a book man. Logistics."

Rey nodded, satisfied. He checked his watch. "I figure we've got another twenty minutes or so, unless they run into trouble on the other level."

Neither man vocalized their definitions of trouble. Mill paced for a while, and Rey sat still in the chair, staring at the wall.

"TRIS, the hatch won't open."

The captain peered down the dim access tube at the white figure on the ladder below him. "All right, go down a little further, then brace yourself so you can have your arms free. We'll probably have to push it open if the power's cut off."

Retter climbed down and cocked his feet against the rungs, locking his legs against the ladder. He watched Tris slide his legs through a rung until he hooked his knees. Retter's breath caught as Tris let go, swinging backward, his face coming within a few inches of his as Tris's back bumped lightly against the ladder.

"You okay?" Tris asked, momentarily distracted by the handsome patient.

Taken aback by the acrobatics, Retter smiled tentatively, fighting the urge to flinch away. "Yeah."

"Let's get this door open, then," Tris said. He punched the wall panel and it flew open. He pulled out some wires and started to twist them together. After a few seconds he paused, looked at Retter, and touched the hatch.

Retter frowned. He'd been studying the older man's reddening face, wondering at Tris's open expressions. "What?"

Tris cleared his throat and went back to the wires. "Just checking." He fiddled a little more and cursed as the wires sparked, but the hatch only slid part-way open. Retter reached out and pushed the panels further apart.

The captain pulled himself upright as Retter climbed out. In short order, they moved down the corridor at a fast clip. Retter accessed the next hatch and stepped through, looking around. Tris followed, and they kept running through the blank metal passageways.

After several minutes, the captain started muttering. "Should be here soon, almost there."

Retter slid to a halt when he saw a tube hatch similar to the one they had exited. "Is this it?"

Tris checked the panel, hit the open button and smiled, patting Retter on the shoulder again. "Good job."

Retter flushed and smiled, secretly thrilled by the other man's touch. "Shall I go first again?"

Tris shook his head. "I'll go, so I can open the hatch up there if it's jammed, too."

Retter quickly yelped in the middle of a nod when a blast from the other end of the hall pushed him into Tris's arms and both of them against the bulkhead.

They peered down the corridor through the haze and sparks. Suddenly Retter jumped and pushed Tris toward the access tube. "In. *In in in* ..." he urged, voice tense, shoving the surprised Tris onto the ladder. "*Move!*" he hissed.

Tris paused in shock. "What..." but he couldn't see past Retter. He started climbing when the patient pushed him again, ducking his own head into the tube at an odd angle.

Tris was barely out of the way when Retter jumped in and hit the access panel, shutting the hatch. Stunned, the captain locked his knees over a ladder rung and swung backwards to hang down again, his face several inches from Retter. "What's..." he asked.

Retter shushed him and pointed toward the hatch. Tris's eyes widened as he looked through the tiny access window.

Armored *things* marched through the corridor. He saw flashes of black and copper, the dull steel of weaponry and an occasional glimpse of shocking blue, a blue not possible in nature. At least the "human" definition of nature.

Retter silently prodded Tris's shoulder, a pleading look on his face. Tris nodded and swung himself up, readjusted his legs and started climbing.

Just as Retter's feet cleared the hatch, weapons' fire obliterated the tube wall and seared through the opposite barrier, just missing his legs. The lasers cut through the steel ladder and left nothing but hissing steam behind – forcing Retter to grip the rungs with both hands as his feet swung free.

Tris tried to get Retter's attention without speaking, but the young man was focused on hanging on. Frustrated, the captain opened the hatch next to him, still one level below where they needed to go, and climbed out. He turned onto his belly and leaned into the hatch, grabbing Retter by the upper arms and wrenching him up and out of the tube.

They rolled out of the access point and Tris hit the button to close the tube hatch, safely closing away the threat of exposure.

Climbing to his knees, he saw Retter curled into a ball, face frozen in fright, eyes glassy. The captain reached out to touch, not thinking.

It was surprising enough to make Retter jerk away violently, out of range.

The captain blinked and his eyes went wide, matching the startled look of horror on Retter's face. Tris looked at his hand and realized what he'd almost done. Retter covered his face with his hands as he struggled for composure, utterly failing as shakes and silent tears broke through.

Tris crawled over and carefully put an arm around his shoulder, letting the patient turn his face away. "It's all right, you're all right." Tris murmured. "I'm all right," he added.

Retter tried to pull away again. Tris let him go and started digging in the medikit he'd slung over his shoulder. He pulled out some latex gloves. "Are these enough?" he blurted out.

Retter looked up at him, his pale, blue-tinged face striped with tears. "Wha... what?"

Tris held up the gloves. "Are these enough protection?"

Retter blinked. "I don't understand."

"Retter. If I put these on, can I touch you safely?" Tris asked, trying to get him to comprehend. He ached to hold the other man, to reassure him that they were safe. He ached to ease his fear.

Retter looked at the gloves and nodded, face scrunching in his confusion. Why would Tris want to touch him?

Tris quickly rolled up his shirtsleeves. He rolled on the gloves carefully, making sure they extended up past his wrists. Then he rolled his sleeves back down, buttoning them.

Retter watched, entranced, tears still running down his face.

Once Tris had the gloves on, he gestured for Retter to come closer. When the patient didn't move, the other man crawled determinedly over and pulled the younger man right into his arms, sitting back and leaning against the hull, holding the trembling body between his knees. Tris wrapped his arms around Retter and lightly stroked a tear-dampened cheek.

After a long moment of hesitation, Retter gave in to his fear and collapsed against him.

MILL practically trembled with nerves as fifteen, then twenty, then thirty minutes passed with no sign of Tris and Retter. Finally he couldn't take it anymore. "Rey, what are we going to do? We can't leave them."

Rey looked up from where he'd been gazing at nothing. "What do you propose, Mill?" he asked dully.

"We can check the access tube at least," Mill said, voice rising.

Rey looked at him and nodded. He stood and moved to the door while Mill rushed out ahead of him. They got to the access point and peered down through the small view port. Rey punched the access numbers and frowned. He punched them again, and the hatch slid open.

Mill ducked his head inside. "Tris?" he called out.

Rey jerked him back inside. "Are you *crazy*? Anybody, *anything* could hear that."

"He didn't answer," Mill said dazedly.

Rey chanced another look into the tube. "I see some light down a couple levels. That's where they should have come in." He squinted. "Looks like the hatch is blown."

Mill stuck his head back into the tube to see, blocking the other man's view. With a muffled oath Rey pulled them both back out.

"All right. So do we go? Or do we stay?" the soldier asked.

Mill frowned. "Go? To the pod? Or down the tube?"

"Or back to the lounge," Rey offered. "We could give them some more time."

"How much time have we got?" Mill asked.

"Man, I've no idea. The ship could blow any minute for all I know. Blue Meanies could come through that corridor. There's no way to tell," Rey said.

Mill took a deep breath and peered back down the tube again. "Why don't I see the ladder?"

Rey frowned. "What?"

"I don't see the ladder – where's the ladder?" Mill asked.

Rey pulled the agitated man out of the tube and looked. Sure enough, where the light flooded the tube, no ladder. "Well, that may be part of the problem."

"Fuck." Mill groaned and covered his eyes, leaning back against the hull.

"You don't have any way to contact Tris? No communicators? No locator beacon?" Rey asked.

Mill shook his head. "All that shit was on the ship. We didn't think we'd need it for a simple unload."

Rey sighed and nodded, closing the hatch. "All right. Come on, let's go sit and think." They returned to the lounge where the soldier once again sat still and Mill paced, muttering.

The seated man wiped his face and shook his head, trying to clear it. "We could try a shipwide broadcast, but then everyone would know where we're going."

Mill continued to pace.

"I could try to get a terminal online and get a heat reading," Rey murmured.

Mill continued to pace.

"Maybe tap out Morse code on some steel pipes?" Rey asked himself, giving the blonde man an annoyed glance.

Mill continued to pace.

With no warning, Mill was plastered against the bulkhead.

The soldier was so close their noses touched. *"Stop. Pacing,"* Rey growled.

Mill growled right back and shoved, only succeeding in moving Rey a few inches. *"Back off!"*

Rey's grip on the other man's jumpsuit tightened and he lifted Mill up against the wall. "You calm the fuck down! You're driving me crazy with your pacing!"

Bristling, Mill pushed against Rey, hands reaching for Rey's as his feet hit the deck. They grappled for control until a shift in balance sent them crashing to the floor.

Mill took advantage and rolled over, pinned Rey's hands down and knelt astride the taller man's hips. He looked down at the snarling face and had to grab hold of Rey's shoulders when the soldier bucked beneath him.

"Get the fuck off," Rey howled. Mill covered his mouth, afraid the yelling would attract notice. But that meant Rey's free hand could cause havoc with Mill's perch, and his hand moved right away. "Mill!" the soldier yelled.

Furious, scared, upset and frustrated, Mill did the first thing that came to mind to silence him. He crushed his mouth against Rey's.

Mill felt the soldier go still under him and Rey's mouth opened, probably to curse at him, which would make more noise, and that was that last thing Mill wanted. So he deepened the impromptu kiss.

At the first touch of Mill's tongue to his lip, Rey froze, shock running rampant through his brain. But his body knew how to respond even if his brain didn't, and the sparks that snapped at his nerve endings made it easy. They clutched each other and the hard kisses turned hungry, desperate, wet, and long. Rey's arms wrapped about Mill and pulled him close; Mill's hands traveled over Rey's shoulders and sides.

Sitting up to gasp for air, Mill looked down at Rey, who propped himself up on his elbows. Mill's hands moved to unseal the top of his own jumpsuit, baring the golden skin underneath to his waist. His flesh bore a thin sheen of sweat. He moved his shaking hands to Rey's jumpsuit and stopped.

Rey trained passion-glazed eyes on Mill and nodded. His lips were swollen and wet from Mill's kisses and he was panting like he'd run the length of the carrier. As soon as Mill had his jumpsuit open, he launched himself up at the other man, sending them backward with a loud thud of rump, knees and elbows as mouths devoured lips, the long line of Rey's neck, the hollow of Mill's collarbone.

The soldier gasped when Mill shifted to suck hard at a stiffened nipple; Mill groaned when Rey moved his hands below the waist, skimming over stiff cotton to palm the stiffer cock underneath.

Rey touched blindly, licking a trail down Mill's body as he pushed their clothing out of the way. When he could stand to separate from Mill for bare seconds, he shifted Mill to his side so they could touch, grip, and squeeze. Rey reached down first, sliding his hand into Mill's jumpsuit and unsealing the fly. Mill swiftly followed, eager to touch more heated skin. Gasps filled their ears as they began to stroke and clutch and pump each other's hardened cock. Their lips moved to crash together as their hips tilted.

Mill felt the heavy cock in his hand twitch and swell, and he bit Rey's lip as the other man groaned in ecstasy while Mill energetically wrung his climax out of him with a tightly curled hand. Mill wasn't far behind. The soldier's calloused hand, the sounds and smell of Rey and the feel of hot come splashing against his own cock pushed him over the edge with a twitch and a bitten lip.

They lay on the carpet, skin steaming, foreheads touching and fabric sticking with their combined sweat. They took a moment and just breathed.

TRIS cradled Retter against him for what seemed like a long time. When the younger man's tears stopped, he kept holding on, giving into the impulse, knowing he wouldn't want to let go. Retter shifted to peer up at Tris, leaning into the crook of his arm. He was sprawled across the captain's lap, the white of his jumpsuit a contrast to the dark, battered leather.

Tris looked down and all he could think was that he held an angel in his arms. He lightly touched the patient's brow and stroked his hair. Retter looked up at him with total acceptance and awe.

Tris's heart swelled to see the shining trust in Retter's eyes, and his gut clenched. "Are you all right now?"

Retter smiled at Tris's soft question. "Yes, thank you," he murmured, reaching up with a glove-covered hand to touch Tris's cheek. His smile grew wider when Tris didn't flinch away. "Thank you."

"It's no big thing."

Retter sobered. "Yes it is."

"I know. I'm sorry. I just didn't want to see you hurting like that." Tris met Retter's questioning gaze. "You captivate me," he whispered.

Retter smiled sadly. "I'm sorry," he whispered. He knew his end was near and that nothing could happen between them. And he regretted it.

Tris shrugged. "It's no big thing."

Retter again boldly stroked his cheek. "Yes – it is."

"Is everything a big thing to you?" Tris joked, trying to lighten the solemnity that had fallen between them.

"When it has to do with touching, yes," Retter replied seriously.

"I guess I can see that. Not too many people would go for that, I imagine; not now," Tris said.

"Not now, not ever," Retter murmured.

Tris frowned. "Ever?"

"I was born with 728PM."

"Born with it? I thought it was a virus from the Bluumeaans," Tris said. Retter nodded. The captain looked him over. "How old are you? I thought Blue Stripes was fatal within five years..."

Retter nodded. "It is, in adult onset. With children, it takes longer. Something about hormones messing with the chemical engineering." He shrugged delicately. "Although for my first eighteen years I had no symptoms, I was kept in quarantine. I'm twenty-five now."

Tris stared at the younger man. "I don't understand."

"I was isolated as I grew up. Everything was conducted by computer, especially once I turned thirteen. The doctors were fairly sure the Blue Stripes would show up once I hit puberty," Retter explained.

"And did it?" Tris had to ask.

"Sort of. They think the engineered virus mutated inside me. There have only been four documented cases. So when I heard about the cure in the works here, I volunteered for the live testing."

"But, if it mutated, are you...? You're still dying?"

Retter met Tris's blue eyes, searching them. He didn't want to give the other man false hope. "I can still infect someone with 728PM. But the virus has done things to me. The doctors told me I could die anytime. The mutation is odd."

Tris snorted. "Hell, I could die at any time. But I didn't give myself up for medical research."

Retter frowned. "Tris, they could beat this disease with my help. I have to take the chance, even if it kills me. It would be saving humanity."

The captain sobered, his gaze absorbed in the deep brown eyes that were so near his own. He nodded slowly, feeling keenly the evanescent opportunity that ghosted through his reach. He couldn't have Retter. Not before, not now, not ever.

Retter smiled heart-breakingly. He would have very much liked to spend more time with Tris, learning and, maybe, loving. "Besides, my life was awfully boring before I met you."

Tris laughed. "I bet." He lightly touched Retter's cheek again, smiling at the way the man seemed to bask in his touch. "So... No touching? At all? Ever?"

"No touching, at all, ever," Retter murmured.

"Not even over your clothes?" Tris asked.

Retter blinked. "What do you mean?"

Tris frowned. "Haven't you been around people at all? How could no one..." he paused, face flushing a bit. It sounded dirty now, to admit he'd thought about practically molesting the other man through his clothes.

"How could no one what?"

"How could no one be around you and not want to touch you?" Tris asked, the question not coming out quite right.

But Retter knew what he meant and he was flattered. The patient shrugged. "They never let anyone close to me. Ever. When you touched my shoulder, that's the second touch I ever remember receiving."

Tris stared at him, his gut clenching with hollow grief. "I'm so sorry."

Retter shrugged, the light in his eyes dimming. "I didn't really know what I was missing, not really..." his voice fell to a whisper. "Until now." He raised his eyes to meet Tris's, the emotion in them staggering.

Tris blinked at him and hugged him closer in response. "When was the first time?"

Retter sighed and leaned his head against Tris's shoulder. "Just before I went into cold storage, the head doctor came into containment and shook my hand, thanking me."

Tris smiled. "That was nice of him."

Retter nodded. "Yes," he whispered.

Tris stroked his glove-covered hand through the patient's curls. He squeezed his eyes shut, trying to talk himself out of what was surely a terrible idea. "Retter, what would you say if I said that I want to touch you?"

Retter chuckled. "Be careful."

Tris grinned, relief crashing through him. "Stinker." He bumped Retter's nose with his knuckle. Then he sighed. "We'd better get moving. Mill and Rey will be worried."

Retter nodded, but didn't move, practically clinging, and Tris found he was loath to let go of the younger man. But he shifted away, breaking the contact, and Retter scrambled to his feet.

Although the ladder going down had been sheared away, the ladder leading up was still solid. Tris checked the access tube carefully, and they quickly climbed to the next level. As Tris pulled himself out of the access tube, Mill came stumbling around the corner, sealing up the front of his jumpsuit. "Tris! Are you okay?"

Tris nodded and turned to take Retter's arms, helping him climb out. "Yeah. Had a close encounter with a squad of Blue Meanies, but we managed to evade them."

Rey stepped around the corner, looking a little mussed. "Glad you guys could join us. We ready to blow this joint?"

Mill accepted a carryall and rifle from Rey and glanced back at Tris and Retter when they started moving. Slowly, he smiled. Then he followed the soldier down the hall.

Retter looked up at Tris. "What was that about?"

Tris shrugged. "No idea."

They followed Mill and Rey, Tris not letting go of Retter's hand.


THE men reached the escape vessel's bay without any more delays. Mill immediately worked to prep the small ship to fly while Rey worked at a terminal, trying to find a safe way to leave the carrier. Retter and Tris stood in the hangar, waiting.

"Where will you go from here?" Retter asked, already feeling a melancholy settle in.

Tris swallowed hard. "I don't know," he answered truthfully, his gaze focused on the man who had captured his heart without even trying. "I think I'll see where life takes me."

The docking bay hatch exploded in without warning, throwing Retter and Tris to the ground, tossing steel and debris against the escape pod. Alarms blared and red lights flared in the chaos.

Rey laid down some cover fire, emptying his rifle before looking for Tris and Retter. "Blue Meanies! We've got to go!" he yelled as he ran over to help them.

Climbing to his feet, Retter looked through the mangled docking bay door. Beyond it, he could see shadowy, moving figures, glimpses of black and copper and that horrifying unnatural blue.

The captain staggered as Rey pulled on him, trying to get him up. Weapons' fire flared through the door, and Rey reeled to the side as he was struck in the shoulder.

Tris lurched to catch his friend, and Retter went to Rey's other side to support him as they threaded through the debris to get to the pod hatch.

Mill's voice came over the intercom. "Move it! We're almost out of time."

Tris glanced back at the door where the Blue Meanies rammed themselves against the steel, trying to get in. Another sizzling-gold bolt of light flashed past his head as he ducked, pushing Rey ahead.

Retter tripped on a burnt piece of steel support, falling to the decking. As Rey stumbled inside the escape pod, Tris returned to help the younger man. He got Retter on his feet and moving again, fatefully glancing back in time to see the attack squad level their weapons again at the docking bay door.

The resulting concussion threw the rest of the door across the bay, chunks of steel and melted slag flying. Tris only had seconds to react as he shielded Retter with his own body, jerking in pain as he bore the brunt of impact.

Retter screamed and tried to pull Tris with him toward the ship. Torn and bloody, the captain stumbled into the vessel behind him, hitting the panel to close the hatch with one fist. He smacked the intercom. "Mill!" he rasped. "Go!"

At the controls, Mill hit the remote and the seal on the bay popped, letting out the air. He watched in satisfaction as the vacuum sucked some of the Blue Meanies into space. Then he hit the engines and piloted the ship out, burning the hell out of whatever was left behind them.

Mill pressed an intercom tab. "Give me five minutes and we're good." He piloted the pod away from the drifting carrier, keeping the hulk between them and the menacing Blue Meanies, and cautiously darted behind a handy asteroid to hide in the string of scanner-deadening rocks. He turned on the autopilot and headed back into the storage section, only to stop still in the hatchway.

Rey sagged against the wall, pale and sweaty, holding his shoulder. He stared at his friend only two meters away.

Tris lay in an expanding pool of blood, the bright red soaking into the white of Retter's jumpsuit and turning to rust. Mill barely suppressed the bile boiling into his throat when he saw the jagged hunk of metal piercing Tris's back and protruding from his stomach.

The captain's hand reached up lightly to touch Retter's cheek, catching a line of silent tears.

Rey dragged himself up and moved to kneel beside them, visually confirming that Tris's midsection was torn all to hell. When Retter looked to him, his eyes pleading, the soldier had to shake his head, clasp Tris's shoulder for a moment, and move away. There was no hope.

Retter turned his gaze back to Tris. "Please, don't leave me when I just found you," he begged.

Tris smiled although his eyes were already glazed. "You're gonna be fine. You're gonna save humanity." A trail of blood dribbled from his brow to slide over his cheek like a teardrop, matching a line of scarlet that fell from the corner of his mouth.

Retter closed his eyes as a wail wrenched free of him. He pulled Tris closer onto his lap. "No, please, I'm the one who's supposed to die. Tris, please..."

"Retter," Tris rasped. "Please, give me a kiss goodbye?"

The patient swallowed back a sob and nodded. Tris reached up to touch his cheek. "Take my glove off. I want to touch you," he murmured, voice already horribly weak.

Hands shaking, Retter stripped the latex glove off and shuddered as Tris's cool fingers touched the soft, wet skin of his cheek. A telltale cobalt blue line skittered under Tris's skin, following the spider web of his veins and blood vessels.

"Now kiss me, Angel, and send me off to sleep. I'll see you soon."

Tears coursing over his cheeks, Retter slid his arms around the captain's shoulders, bowed his head and kissed him with all his heart. Tris's lips moved against his in silent words before he pressed close with one last bit of strength.

And then Tris sagged away and Retter sat trembling, staring at Tris's unmoving, blue-tinged face.

Before anyone could take another breath, the ship tipped to the side as it was hit from outside. Rey jerked out of his trance and lurched to the cockpit, yelling for Mill to come with him.

Mill stumbled out of the storage section, sparing a last glance for Tris's body, sheltered in Retter's arms. He entered the cockpit and sat next to Rey.

"So, Book Man, I don't suppose you can fly?" Rey asked, hurriedly hitting buttons.

"Some, yeah... Tris taught me." Mill swallowed the burst of despair that threatened.

"Well, dredge it up. Try to avoid the worst of those volleys. This little pod has a few bells and whistles I can pull out," Rey said.

"Who the fuck are you, man?" Mill asked, surprised. "Soldier, doctor, scientist, munitions ..."

Rey's face was pinched with pain, his arm hanging limp from a shoulder crusted with black and muddy rust. He stretched and flinched, then tried again, and turned on the laser sights. "Get to flying," was his curt response.

Mill gulped and took the controls, some of the maneuvers Tris had used coming back to him as he veered around the worst of what the three fighters threw at them. What did get through gave the ship a good rocking.

Rey cursed and hit more buttons, trying to get the computer to cooperate.

"What's the problem?" Mill asked frantically.

"I'm trying to get a scientific pod to let me use some of its toys as weapons and the computer doesn't quite get it. It's going to take me a few minutes."

"We may not have a few minutes!" Mill yelped as the vessel took a solid hit to the rear.

Rey kept hitting buttons and typing commands with one hand. He smiled grimly as he got a green light. "All right, Mill, face us toward one of those ships."

Mill shook his head in disbelief but did as Rey requested. A Bluumeaan fighter was bearing down on them when Rey hit a couple of buttons.

All the lights in the pod flickered for a moment, and then stabilized. Mill blinked and looked at the fighter. Then he swore and hit the controls, swerving the ship out of the way as the fighter flew by on momentum, skewed, all its power gone.

"What'd you do?" Mill asked, glancing over at Rey, who was again frantically punching buttons.

"Electromagnetic burst. Fried all the computers. Unfortunately, I need a few minutes before I can do it again without killing us, too," Rey said.

"Well, don't kill us too!" Mill answered heatedly, a tinge of panic in his voice. The ship listed drunkenly as it was hit from behind.

"Fuck, Mill – don't let them blow us up," Rey yelled.

"Christ, Rey, whadda you want me to do?" Mill asked, frantically steering, trying to shake the fighters off the ship's tail.

"Shit! We've got a hull breach in the back," Rey muttered as a high-pitched alarm keened.

"Hull breach?" Mill parroted, sweat trailing from his temples.

"We've got to stabilize or we're going to lose the engines. I'm going to have to go back there," Rey said.

"Go back there? I need you here! You have to kill those Blue Meanies!" Mill yelled.

"Half dozen one way, six the other," Rey ground out as he typed quickly into the terminal. He grabbed for the control console and pulled off the door, revealing the wiring.

"Now what?" Mill yelled as the ship shuddered under another volley of fire.

"Damn it, turn around and keep him beside us or in front of us. If he hits us at the hull breach it'll incinerate the ship," Rey yelled back.

The soldier twisted some wires, cussed them, bit the plastic covering off a couple more and pinched them together, then climbed back up to the terminal.

"All right, Mill, full stop," Rey said.

Mill took a deep breath and cut the engines. He heard the groan of the hull right away.

Rey winced. "All right, they've got to get close for this to work."

Mill frowned as Rey turned off all the power, the lights, anything moving. The Bluumeaan ships drifted closer, guns trained on the small vessel, sensing an easy kill.

"Yeah, we're just a dead little ducky," Rey rasped.

"Dead little ducky hissing air," Mill added nervously.

"Just a little closer..." Rey wiped his anxious face, hand cramping over the keyboard. Suddenly he hit the keys and the ship flared to life, only to flicker again and die down to a low hum.

Mill watched as the other ships went dark in a sizzle and a spark, leaving them alone behind the planetoid. "Thank God."

Rey jerked to climb past him. "Got to stop that breach or we're gonna die..." he stopped and blinked when the alarm shut itself off. He leaned over to check the board. "Huh. The bulkhead sealed. Retter must have..."

"See, Mill, I told you that you were getting good at piloting."

Mill and Rey looked up from their seats to see Tris standing in the doorway with Retter under his arm supporting him. They gaped at the man who stood in the doorway grinning like a loon.

"I sealed that breach before it killed us. You really ought to be more careful, Rey. I thought you had a better handle on keeping a ship intact than that," Tris teased.

Mill scrunched up his face and shook his head. "You... You bastard! You're alive!"

Tris grinned. "Yeah!"

Rey opened his mouth to speak and shut his jaw closed without making a sound, his eyes darting down to Tris's midsection. Retter chuckled.

Mill looked at Rey. "The man says 'yeah.' He was dead. On the floor. In a puddle of his own blood. And he says, 'yeah'?" Tris chuckled as Mill stood up angrily only to bang his head on the metal overhang and drop like a stone, cussing.

Retter laughed aloud. "Are you okay?"

Mill cursed again and stood up – carefully this time – edging away from the consoles to stand in front of them. He leaned over to touch Tris's miraculously healed midsection, but the captain stepped back.

"Best not, Mill, not yet, anyway," Tris said.

Mill frowned. "What? Why?"

Tris held up his hand. Rey and Mill could clearly see his veins standing out, faded blue against the paler skin of his palm. "Blue Stripes!" Mill yelped, cringing back without thinking.

Tris nodded and lowered his hand, smoothing it over his belly. Mill stared. There wasn't a mark on him, not anywhere that he could see. The man had been shredded by shrapnel. And now he was whole?

"Tris, I don't... What...?" Mill asked, dumbfounded.

"I don't know how or why, but when Retter touched me and transmitted the Blue Stripes, it healed me," Tris explained.

Rey's eyes grew very large and wide. Retter hugged Tris close to him. Tris looked down at him with a smile. "How do you feel?" Rey asked carefully.

"Feel?" Tris asked, shrugging, "Fine. Actually, I feel great. Better than I have in a long time."

Mill studied him. The man he'd always known to slouch was standing up straight, and his face... "Tris, your wrinkles are gone."

Tris's hand flew to his face. "What?"

"And your hair's not gray anymore," Retter murmured. The soldier muttered to himself, patting his pockets.

Tris looked down in wonder at his palm. Retter hugged him as Rey cleared his throat. They all looked over to see him holding up a data chip.

"These are the last results of the research," Rey said. "The last batch of patients, including Retter, they were the only four mutated cases of 728PM we could find. Anywhere. We needed them to test the results of the transmission of the mutated disease, with both original cases of Blue Stripes and unaffected individuals."

They all goggled at Rey. "How do you know so much? And again I ask, who the fuck are you?" Mill asked.

Rey had the decency to look abashed.

"He's the head of the entire research project," Retter said quietly.

Mill looked back and forth between Retter and Rey. "What?"

Rey spoke up. "I'm not a medical doctor," he quickly clarified. "I'm the military scientist they put in charge of the doctors."

Tris grinned. "I always knew you'd do good, Techie."

Rey rolled his eyes. "Oh hell no, no one calls me that anymore."

Mill frowned. "How long have you known Rey, Tris?"

"He was in boot camp with me. Young whiz kid," the captain answered as Rey grinned at him.

Mill's eyes bulged. "Boot camp? You were in boot camp?"

A homing beacon interrupted them and Rey turned to the display as a friendly ship sailed into view, hailing them. He opened the channel and welcomed them in relief.

*[Four weeks later]*


REY grinned as he walked into the exam room with Mill; a whole and healthy Tris waved from the patient's chair. They joined him, staying quiet until the nurse finished with the charts and left them alone.

"How are you, Tris?" Mill asked solemnly. It was the first time he'd gotten to see the captain since he was whisked away right after they were rescued.

Tris extended his hand to Mill so the other man could see the blue-tinged veins. "I'm still here," he said to his friend.

"So now what? You're all healed up, but you can't touch anyone?" Mill asked.

Tris shrugged. "All healed up with my own special little version of Blue Stripes. Benefits included." He waggled his eyebrows from his place in the chair.

"Special version? Benefits?" Mill echoed, sitting down an arm's length him before looking to Rey, who leaned against the wall.

"Health benefits," Rey clarified. "Better vision, better hearing, more efficient body functions – simply *better*. And younger. It's amazing."

Tris smiled when Mill shook his head. "So what's it mean?"

Rey leaned forward. "What it means is that Retter's mutated Blue Stripes can heal anyone of damn near anything. We tested extensively. He even cures the original Blue Stripes."

Mill stared at him in shock. "And these people who are healed, they all become like Tris?"

Rey nodded. "And people like you, Mill, who aren't hurt, aren't sick, if we expose you to Retter or to someone he's touched, you get your own version of human Blue Stripes vaccine." He smiled widely and held up his own palm, where blue traced under the skin.

"Vaccine! That's *incredible!*" Mill exclaimed.

Rey nodded. "It's a goddamn miracle. And it gets better. If you're vaccinated, you can spread that vaccine to anyone else."

Mill leaned back, overwhelmed. "So this means..."

"It means we've beaten Blue Stripes, Mill," Tris said quietly. "We've beaten illness. Disease. Injury. At least for now. Who knows what will happen in the future?"

"Humans and the diseases that prey upon us will continue evolving," Rey said. "Nature created its own vaccine for a disease that was engineered to wipe us out." He chuckled. "Actually, in a way, the Blue Meanies gave us an edge. They can't really hurt us now."

Mill leaned back and shook his head. "It's a lot to take in." Then he noticed Tris was alone. "Where's Retter? He's okay, right?" he asked, looking around. He'd figured the younger man would be stuck to Tris's side.

Rey chuckled. "He's fine. He's in the hospital children's ward, infecting every sick kid he can find." They all grinned.

"He's due here any minute," Tris said, sitting on the edge of the chair, eyes darting to the door.

Rey rolled his eyes. "They've been separated the past two weeks while we ran Tris through the wringer. Couldn't have the results skewed."

Mill leaned forward, eyes narrowing. "So Tris, what's this about boot camp? You never told me you were in the service."

Tris colored a bit and ducked his head. "I, ah, don't talk about it much."

Rey snickered. Mill looked over to him. "What?"

"They bought out his enlistment," Rey said conspiratorially.

"What?" Mill asked in alarm.

Tris rolled his eyes. "They couldn't teach me anything about flying, so they bought me out and sent me off. Said I was a bad influence."

"You are a terrible influence."

All three men looked up as Retter breezed into the room with a wide grin on his face. Mill chuckled. Taking advantage of his newfound freedom, Retter was wearing cutoff trousers and a short-sleeved T-shirt.

Tris stood and Retter stopped a few feet from him, their eyes locking.

Mill and Rey looked at one another and with matching nods, both stood. "We'll see you two later!" They fled the room with good-natured haste.

Tris and Retter stared at one another for several seconds before Tris reached out and pulled Retter against him, enveloping him in a hug.


OUTSIDE the door, Rey stopped, catching Mill's attention. "Have you thought about what you'll do next?" the soldier asked hesitantly, shoving his hands in his pockets.

Shaking his head, Mill crossed his arms. "I haven't been able to talk to Tris until today, of course, and I figure..." he glanced back at the door, "I won't talk to him for at least a couple more days."

"Decided you're staying with him, then?" Rey prodded.

"Hadn't really thought about it. Why?" Mill asked.

Rey's tongue darted out ever so slightly, tracing his lip. "A research lab has reopened right here and I get to corral the whole damn thing. I could use a man with a good head for numbers," he said.

Mill studied him, fascinated that the soldier-turned-scientist seemed so off-kilter. "Opportunity for advancement?" he asked.

"Considering you'd be starting out working for the boss, there's not much further up you can go," Rey said, leaning against the wall. "But there will be other benefits." He shifted awkwardly on his feet.

Indicating his question by arching an eyebrow, Mill suspected he knew what the other man was hinting at, but he waited until Rey chanced a glance up.

"Room and board in the new scientific facility, good pay, commensurate with your last active rank plus experience, of course medical and emergency benefits..." Rey shifted yet again, keeping his head down. "And then there's Blue Stripes. And me."

"Blue Stripes. And you," Mill repeated evenly, despite the smile on his face. He willed the other man to look up at him.

Rey finally met Mill's eyes and the worry drained away as he saw the amusement and affection there. "Bastard," the soldier muttered, shaking his head.

Mill grinned and slid his arms around Rey's waist, pressing close against his chest. "Where do I sign up?" he asked huskily, then pressed his lips to Rey's in a firm kiss. Deep blue twisted its way under Mill's skin, flooding his veins and blood vessels with vaccine. All Mill felt was the warmth in Rey's arms.

ALONE in Medical, Retter sighed happily and wrapped himself around Tris, hanging off him like a limpet. Even though

Retter was light, the movement threw Tris off balance and he sat in the chair abruptly.

Retter straddled Tris's lap, bracing his knees on the heavy leather under them. He twined his arms about Tris's neck. "Tris, I think I love you."

Tris blinked, then his face transformed with a huge smile and he chuckled, wrapping his arms about Retter's waist. "Well, I certainly hope so, because I know I love you."

Retter grinned and leaned forward to steal a kiss.

Tris stroked his fingers through Retter's curls, reveling in the opportunity to touch openly and as often as he liked. "What would you say if I said that I want to touch you?"

Retter chuckled, remembering the first time Tris asked that question. "Be my guest," was his answer this time. He reached out and took Tris's hand, placing the palm against the warm skin of his neck.

Tris grinned and pulled Retter's mouth to his, their lips meeting in a passionate kiss. Retter wrapped himself around the other man, and Tris's hands tried to touch every bit that he could.

Retter moaned into his mouth. "Tris, please, love me..."

Tris chuckled and stripped off Retter's T-shirt, throwing it aside. "Oh, I plan to... And well."

Retter started grabbing at Tris's clothes, baring his chest and opening his trousers right where he sat in the chair. With a minimum of fuss, the younger man moved, stripped and climbed right back onto Tris's lap. The older man wrapped both their cocks in his hands, groaning as they slid together.

Retter tipped his head back and let out a long moan of approval, pushing into Tris's fist. Tris responded by sucking Retter's neck and pumping his throbbing cock, grinning as he elicited another needy groan. He earned several more of those groans over the next long minutes.

"Tris... I'm so close already... so close," Retter keened, hands scrabbling to hold on to Tris's shoulders. "Missed you, missed you."

"Then come for me, baby, and I'll use your come to slick my way when I fuck you," Tris growled into his ear.

Thrilled, Retter gasped as his gut clenched and he howled when his cock throbbed in Tris's hands. His body jerked against his lover's. Tris pulled Retter against his chest and slid his come-wet fingers down to his lover's ass, pressing in and wetting the way for his cock, which now ached terribly.

Retter whimpered and wiggled against Tris's fingers, his own cock hardening again at the stimulation from the fingers inside him. "So incredible..." he breathed eagerly.

Tris grinned. "Up on your knees for a bit, lover," he urged, helping Retter raise himself so he could get his cock lined up. "Now, slowly," and he guided the younger man down onto him.

Retter cried out as Tris' arousal breached him, but after a gulp of air he relaxed, a smile growing on his face as he sank onto Tris, garnering a groan of pleasure from his more experienced lover.

"Isn't that how it's supposed to work?" Retter asked as he wiggled around a bit, thrilled by the feeling of Tris seated deep within him. It was only their third time together.

Tris groaned again. "Thank God for all those years of research you did."

Retter laughed delightedly and started moving, fucking himself on Tris, and within spare minutes they were both wild, Tris's hands on Retter's hips, goading him into faster, sharper movements.

"Oh *baby*, oh Retter..." Tris gasped for breath as he exploded inside his lover, his vision turning to stars, his ears filled with Retter's own cry of pleasure. He felt his belly warm and wet with Retter's come.

The younger man leaned against Tris's chest with a sigh, snuggling close. "What will you do now?"

"I hear there's a brand new hero of humanity who needs to fly all over creation and touch people," Tris murmured, pinching Retter's ass.

Retter sat up, looking at Tris seriously. "You're the hero here."

Tris's lips twitched and he stole another kiss. "Don't tell anyone. You'll ruin my image."

# FOLLOWING THE SUN

GROANING, he pushed himself upright from where he lay over the burnt and blackened control panel. He took stock of the myriad aches and pains shooting through him before he glanced around carefully, looking for his companion in the dark interior of the small cockpit.

"Samuel?" he called out, his usually soft voice a hoarse rasp. When he heard no answer, he struggled to his feet, hissing and holding his injured arm against his chest. Grimacing, he figured it was broken. It could have been much worse, he thought ruefully. Looking around at the complete destruction, it really should have been. When he shifted his weight a sharp pain streaking along his leg made him peer down and he could see a long, ragged tear through his blood-crusted trousers. No wonder he hurt so badly.

Stumbling out of the steel-gray cockpit of the shuttle, he leaned heavily against the flat, featureless wall as he made his way to the cargo bay, noting the sunlight pouring in through rents in the craft. Blinking in disbelief, he shook his head, amazed to be alive after the violent crash-landing from space.

But he really stopped to stare when he found the heavy bulkhead hatch open. An explosion of verdant green surrounded the ship, lush trees rising far above the crippled vessel, the ground covered with vines and smaller plants erupting with riotous color. Birds flew about in the bright sunshine that poured into the jungle along the path the craft had torn through the lush canopy.

"Jack, you're awake!"

Shading his eyes, Jack looked out to see Samuel approaching from outside the ship, sun glinting off his short-cropped blond hair and pale skin. "You all right?" Jack asked, leaning heavily on the hatch.

"Yeah, a little banged up. You hit your head, though, and were out cold, so I left you where you were and went looking for signs of civilization. No luck," Samuel shrugged as he stopped to stand knee-high in plants. "You'd think if I had to crash, I could have done it near a city."

"Hell, Samuel, we were lucky to even find a planet, much less a city on the planet," Jack said shortly, sinking to sit down, cradling his arm, taking pressure off his leg.

"Yeah, I know. We lost the navigational while in hyper — we could have come out anywhere. We were lucky," Samuel murmured, stopping next to his longtime friend and sometime lover. "Is your arm broken?"

Jack nodded, looking a little ill as he sagged against the bulkhead. "Yeah. Hurts like hell."

Samuel climbed up the damaged wing of the shuttle to the hatch and moved past Jack nimbly. "Let me get the First Aid kit, and we'll see if I can patch you up."

Not moving from where he leaned against the frame of the door, Jack gazed into the jungle, exhausted. He could make out every color green imaginable and more, not to mention patches of color. Flowers, he thought. Fruit, more birds, the entire jungle seemed to be moving and shifting, teeming with life. Blearily he tried to focus closer, peering at the dust motes dancing in the unblocked ray of sunshine that enveloped him. He dragged a bloody hand through his hair, leaving a streak of red along his temple.

A moving shadow caught the man's attention and he turned his head to see... nothing. Closing his eyes for a moment, Jack decided shaking his head wouldn't be a good idea. Obviously he'd suffered a concussion, his eyes could barely stay focused, and he knew he'd be better off staying awake for now. Dragging his eyes open, another shifting shadow pulled at his attention, but when he looked he saw nothing there. The shimmering waves of warmth streaming from the verdant vegetation gave him an uneasy sense of vertigo.

"All right – we got painkillers, we got transderm patches, we got antibiotics," Samuel said as he crouched next to Jack, startling him. Samuel tilted up his chin, looking at his deep blue eyes critically. "You really took a hit to the head." His light-skinned fingers lingered on Jack's ruddy skin, stroking gently.

"Yeah," Jack rasped, reaching to wipe away a bead of sweat, fingers tangling in his short, messy, sandy brown hair, smearing the blood. The humidity and warmth of the jungle seeped into him, making him even sleepier. "I keep seeing things moving out of the corner of my eye. Just shadows, the trees blowing or a bird or something, but it's bad enough I can't focus on any one thing."

"Let me give you a couple of these shots, and then I'll see about your leg and arm," Samuel said, going to work as Jack leaned against the bulkhead.

Peering again into the green, Jack's mind wandered and he admired the rays of sunshine, thankful he was alive at all. The warmth here contrasted sharply with the freezing cold of space that often leeched through into the ship. He relaxed a little more as the painkiller shot kicked in. Jack didn't blink any more when shadows moved boldly across his vision. In fact, the hazy form outlined in the sunshine didn't really register either as he looked at it fully, his mind not comprehending.

Muttering, Samuel did his best to patch Jack up. He covered the long gash in his friend's leg with transderm patches, though he couldn't do much with the arm but wrap it tightly and hope the bones lined up right. It could be fixed once they returned to civilization. If they made it back to civilization, he thought darkly. Samuel glanced up at the other man, seeing the dull stare, and frowned. Out of morbid curiosity he glanced over his shoulder to see if Jack actually saw anything. He froze in place, shocked.

A tall man, lean and muscular, stood about fifty feet away, silhouetted in the sunshine, his front in shadow. He wore breeches of rough material, some sort of belt slung about his hips and another about his chest. His bronzed arms and torso, both bare, bore stripes of paint tracked with sweat. His sharp-boned face, surrounded by a mane of long, sun-burnished brown hair, also bore marks of the heated humidity. Leather ties strapped a large knife to each thigh, and he supported a tall spear in long-fingered hands.

Samuel swallowed and glanced to Jack, whose eyes appeared glazed. He carefully shook the other man's shoulder. "C'mon, Jacky, snap out of it, we have a visitor." Then he glanced up again. "Visitors," he corrected nervously.

Jack's eyes slid closed as he tried to get his mind to focus on his surroundings. When he pulled them open again, several men stood not too far away, all in various states of tribal-style dress. "Samuel?" Jack asked weakly.

Gripping his friend's shoulder to reassure him, Samuel stood, looking around at the men. The one still standing in the sun was the tallest and wore the most markings, and Samuel figured by his bearing that he led this band of warriors. The pilot rubbed his sweaty palms on his torn trousers and held up his hands, palms up, in a sign of peace, as he put his broad-shouldered body between Jack and the natives.

A quiet murmur passed through the armed men, and Samuel watched them all step back so that a slim man wearing a long, flowing tunic could approach. Watching him carefully, Samuel made no forward move as he studied the golden-skinned, wiry figure that approached, seeing a strong-featured face come out of shadow. He figured he could fight him, but he hoped to avoid that, especially since the muscled man on the rise watched him closely. They needed help and he'd take what he could get, if only for Jack's sake.

Jack watched the native stop a few feet away as he drew a deep breath and forced himself to stand, pushing himself up, still holding his arm. He wavered on his feet, though, and nearly yelped in surprise when the man reached out to steady him with a firm but solicitous grip on his good elbow. Samuel almost reacted badly when the native reached out to take Jack's arm, but managed to stop his frantic response.

His smaller frame made this man less a threat, with his finer-boned structure and almost pretty tanned skin. Dark curls framed his face and brushed his shoulders. He looked over them both with animated dark brown eyes, studying them keenly, then said something over his shoulder. The voice rippled musically, a soft burr speaking a lyrical language. One of the other men stepped up and handed him a bag by its strap.

Jack watched, brow furrowing a bit until the native tilted up the bag to his mouth, drinking a bit of the liquid that poured out. Then looking at the both of them, he held up the bag. "San van tahla," he said, offering the bag to Jack.

Jack glanced to Samuel, who shrugged very slightly. Nodding, Jack accepted the bag, finding it heavy with liquid. He carefully raised it one-handed and took a nervous sip, utter relief filling him when he tasted pure water. He took several long gulps and offered the bag to Samuel with a smile. "It's water," he said.

Samuel smiled and drank as well, then offered the bag back to the man in the tunic. "Thank you," he said clearly, bowing his head.

The observer standing a bit further away, still stoic, relaxed slightly as the slim man in front of them bowed in return, taking the bag. After a few more words, a smile, and a wave from the man with the water, chattering warriors waving their hands in an attempt to communicate surrounded Samuel and Jack.

The injured spacer sagged weakly, unable to believe their luck. Samuel also looked relieved, although he kept an eye on the tall leader, who stepped a bit closer out of the bright sun, studying them. He could make out his strong face now, and darting eyes that kept close tabs on the scene. Some of the painted lines Samuel could now identify as scars. The man was obviously a fighter.

Within a few minutes, the man who spoke to them gave some obvious orders to the others, and they talked amongst themselves briefly before falling silent and looking to the leader. He nodded. The warriors took off, disappearing into the trees like mist, silent. Samuel and Jack watched in awe, unable to track the men through the foliage.

The warrior stepped forward and with one hand beckoned them to follow. Samuel looked to Jack, who gave him a helpless look.

"I'm going to grab a couple of bags, just to be safe," Samuel said, making a "wait" motion with his hands. His jump-suited figure disappeared into the darkness of the ship.

Jack sank down to sit again, his feet dangling a few feet from the ground. When he looked up, the slim native stood next to him and pointed to his arm.

"It's broken," Jack rasped, grimacing in pain.

Placing the water bag on the craft's wing, the native held out his hands as if to touch, waiting for Jack's permission. Not sure what the man wanted, Jack nodded, using the chance to study the native more closely.

His skin gleamed with a thin sheen of sweat as if oiled, and he wore an open blue robe trimmed with gold over loose trousers to cover a lithe, lightly muscled body. A leather thong hung about his neck, weighted by a piece of copper beaten into a representation of a shining sun. He seemed younger than the others and bright-eyed, Jack noted distractedly. It made him feel old, broken down and out of shape with the several extra pounds he'd gained before this supply run gone wrong.

The native started at Jack's shoulder, feeling along the shirt-covered arm, pressing gently but thoroughly. Jack hissed and went white when he prodded the break, and the man said a few words under his breath and started unwrapping Jack's arm. Next he pulled out his knife, and before Jack could say a word, he split the sleeve of the spacer's gray flight suit from wrist to shoulder.

Samuel stopped in the door, heart pounding and tree-green eyes wide as he watched. The native glanced at Jack and raised a brow. Confused, Jack frowned. Then the man jerked his arm with some force and Jack yelled, nearly blacking out. Samuel jumped down next to the native, yelling as well.

Ignoring Samuel, the man prodded at Jack's arm again and nodded, still muttering, and started to rewrap the arm. Jack, pale again, gasped for breath and opened his eyes. "Samuel, leave him alone. I think he fixed my arm."

Looking doubtful, Samuel watched the man finishing wrapping. "You sure about that, Jacky?"

"Yeah, the pain's already fading," Jack said. "Now I'm just exhausted."

As soon as those words left his mouth, two natives appeared from the trees carrying a stretcher. Samuel saw it and chuckled. "Well look – great service here," he joked, the exhaustion catching up with him also as adrenaline drained away.

Jack raised a bushy brow and laughed weakly. "Think we'll get room service?"

The leader waiting to one side looked between the two laughing strangers and shook his head, although a tiny smile pulled at the corners of his mouth. He picked up one of the large bags Samuel brought and gestured for the healer to take the other as Samuel helped Jack onto the stretcher.

As they walked into the jungle, Samuel looked back at the cratered shuttle, suddenly wondering if he'd ever see it again.

THE muscled warrior called another halt, and Samuel sat on a large rock, huffing for breath. Though he wasn't by any means overweight, his heavier bones and stout build made exertion like this difficult. It was one reason he preferred outer space.

The men carrying Jack trailed a bit farther behind, taking their time moving through the underbrush, accompanied by the slim man.

Swallowing, Samuel tried to remember what the man said back at the ship. "Sanantall?" he muttered, looking at the dirt. "Zanantahl?"

"San van tahla."

Samuel glanced up, seeing the watcher crouching a few feet away. The crisscrossing scars and swaths of paint decorated his body. More paint slashed across his cheekbones and beneath it, Samuel could see a firm jaw and intelligent eyes. The skin exposed to air gleamed with sweat.

"Sonvon talle," Samuel attempted to mimic.

Tilting his head, the man's eyes glinted with humor, and he said the words again, slowly. "San van tahla."

"San van tahla," Samuel repeated, much closer this time. Nodding, the native pulled a strap over his head and offered the water bag to Samuel, who accepted it gratefully. After several swallows, Samuel sighed and handed the bag back. "Thank you."

"Taank ewe," the warrior parroted.

Blinking, Samuel grinned. He repeated the words slowly, pressing his hands together and bowing slightly to convey meaning. "Thank you."

"Taank yewe," he said slower, eyes narrowing as he repeated.

Samuel nodded. "Thank you."

The tall man smiled slightly and touched his chest. "Arl'ban."

"Is that your name? Arrbuin?" Samuel asked, relaxing a little on the rock, rubbing the sweat from his forehead.

Tapping his chest again, the man nodded. "*Arrrrlll*bahhn. Arl'ban."

"Arl'ban. Got it. I'm Samuel," the spacer answered, tapping his own chest.

Arl'ban frowned. "Ayyeahmsmmel."

Snorting, Samuel shook his head, telling himself to be more specific. He tapped his chest. "Samuel."

"Shahmwoll," Arl'ban repeated, peering at him curiously. "*Sahm*well."

Bobbing his head, Samuel smiled. "Yeah. Samuel."

"Taank yewe, Sahmwell," Arl'ban tried out the foreign words.

Chucking, Samuel nodded. "San van tahla. Arl'ban."

The man made to hand back the water bag, but Samuel shook his head. Arl'ban blinked in realization and he nodded, tapping the bag. "Tahla."

"Water," Samuel said. "Tahla."

"Wahtuh. Tahla," Arl'ban answered, fascinated. "Wahtuh."

Samuel nodded and pointed to the native. "Arl'ban." Then he pointed to the bag. "Tahla."

The warrior broke into a wide smile so unlike his earlier self, striking Samuel speechless. Strong white teeth and full, red lips – and the spacer swallowed hard on sudden burgeoning desire.

Arl'ban tilted his head. "Wahtuh?" he asked, holding out the bag.

Samuel accepted the bag and took a drink, using the time to recover himself. Handing it back he said, "Thank you."

"Simi san."

Samuel peered at the other man. "See me san?"

Arl'ban pressed his hands together and bowed slightly in a perfect mimic of Samuel's earlier movements. "Simi san."

Samuel nodded and bowed slightly. "Simi san."

"What are you two chattering on about?"

Samuel glanced up, surprised as Arl'ban jerked back and stood up, stepping away, suddenly back to the stoic warrior. The spacer looked to see Jack half sitting up in the stretcher as the two natives carrying him paused several feet away. "Hey, Jacky, how are you feeling?"

"Awful, but that's better than I was. Did you strike up a conversation?" Jack asked, curious. The younger native stood next to him, a thoughtful smile on his face.

"Uh, yeah. This is Arl'ban," Samuel said, gesturing to the warrior who listened carefully.

"Arl'ban, huh? Well, I hope you thanked him for his hospitality," Jack said tiredly as he lay back down, carefully arranging his long legs.

"Simi san," Samuel said, unknowingly drawing a slight smile from Arl'ban.

"What's that?" Jack asked.

"I'm pretty sure it's thank you," the blond spacer replied.

Turning his head to look at Arl'ban, Jack nodded obviously. "Simi san," he said. The man surprised him by offering a half bow in return.

Arl'ban said several words to the porters, and they moved Jack again. Samuel stood up to follow, but Arl'ban caught his arm and gestured for him to follow a different way. Wary and not happy about being separated from his friend in the darkening jungle, Samuel followed him for a few minutes through the heavy underbrush, only stopping when Arl'ban's arm blocked his way.

"What the...?" Samuel swore under his breath – the warrior was not even a foot away, and they were of a size, both tall and wide, bodies tapering down from their shoulders. Then Arl'ban moved the wide fronds from in front of their faces.

They stood on the side of a mountain, looking down into a heavily forested gully. Samuel easily could make out the scar torn through the trees by their crash landing, although he could barely see the ship in the distance. Arl'ban tapped his arm and pointed the opposite direction.

Samuel gasped as he saw they stood on the edge of some sort of city hidden in the trees except for a tall pyramid of stone that rose from the jungle. The city spread through the trees, a part of the wilds, myriad lights blinking out through the mists. Stunned, Samuel figured there must be thousands upon thousands of lights filling the valley.

"Lan'do'tay," Arl'ban said.

"It's beautiful," Samuel breathed.

Arl'ban smiled, understanding the sentiment if not the words. "Chimi," he said, beckoning for Samuel to follow. With one last look over his shoulder, Samuel did.

THE gentle rocking of the stretcher and then warm darkness lulled Jack into a light doze until he felt the litter lowered onto something soft and giving. He pulled his eyes open to look up at a stone ceiling. Blinking, he looked around.

The porters laid the stretcher across a pallet of soft material on a platform in a simple stone room. Torches burned on the wall, lighting the area with golden warmth. Several baskets lined the far wall. Pushing himself to sit up, Jack blinked as a man appeared in the doorway – the slighter one who talked to them at the ship.

He approached and lightly touched the back of his hand to Jack's forehead. "San van tahla?" he asked, his voice soft and soothing.

Blinking, Jack remembered that he had heard those words before. He nodded. The man reached over into a basket and pulled out a familiar water bag and offered it to him. Jack took a long draught, then sighed and held it out. "Simi san," he said.

The man smiled widely, brightening his features. Jack swallowed again at the blinding beauty before him, frozen as the man perched on the side of the bed and started running his hands over Jack's leg. His body reacted although his mind could barely believe. It took him a long moment to realize he wasn't being felt up. The man was merely checking the wound on his leg. Jack squeezed his eyes shut and bit his lip on a soft moan. Being this close made him wish for better looks than his plain, homely face presented.

Soft, questioning words made Jack open his eyes. The man peered at him, head tilted in question, concern easily read in his eyes. *He must be asking if I'm okay*, Jack thought.

"I'm fine," he said, easing himself back onto one elbow. "Simi san."

The man sat back, looking like he didn't quite believe him, but he didn't know how to communicate it.

Jack looked up him, at a loss. He decided to try what Samuel said he tried with Arl'ban. He tapped his chest. "Jack."

The man cocked his head, eyes curious. "Juhahk."

The spacer smiled. "Yes. Jack."

"Jahk," the man repeated, smiling. Then he tapped his own chest. "Lan'do."

"That's an easy one. Lan'do," Jack said, relieved he didn't have to sound it out like Arl'ban.

Lan'do nodded. "Lan'do," he said, gesturing to himself, "Jahk," he said, pointing to the reclining man. "San van tahla, Jahk?" he asked, offering the water bag.

Jack shook his head. "No, simi san, Lan'do."

"Dran, simi san," the native said.

He offered the bag again, and Jack considered. He shook his head again. "Dran, simi san." Smiling, Lan'do nodded and set the bag aside. Jack chuckled. This was going better than he could have hoped. He wondered about Samuel. "Lan'do? Where is Samuel?"

Lan'do patted Jack's knee. "Sahmwell marshallus," he said and then paused, frowning. He settled for placing his hands together, laid his cheek against them, and closed his eyes.

"Oh, he's sleeping. I get it. Simi san," Jack said, relaxing.

Lan'do nodded. "Marshallus a Arl'ban getana."

Jack chuckled. "I'll assume that means he's sleeping at Arl'ban's rather than with Arl'ban." He snickered a little before he could stop himself. Apparently, Lan'do understood, because he chuckled as well. The soft laugh from Lan'do made Jack snort again, and his tired laughter broke free. He lay back with a sigh, still chuckling, when he peered up at the other man.

Lan'do grinned down at him, eyes sparkling. He shifted and stood, moving to the foot of the bed and picking up a bowl on the floor, carrying it back with him. He sat closer to Jack's chest this time and offered what looked like a piece of fruit.

The spacer focused on the dripping chunk in Lan'do's fingers. "Do I eat it?" Jack asked, motioning to his mouth.

Lan'do nodded and popped the piece of fruit into his mouth, chewing with a smile. Then he reached into the bowl and offered another piece to Jack. "Prangn?"

Jack reached out for the fruit, stopping when he saw his hands filthy with dirt, burns and blood. He frowned and held up his hand. "Tahla?" he asked, wanting to wash the mess away.

Lan'do nodded and set the bowl in the floor, walking over to a basket and pulling out another bowl and a cloth. He filled the bowl with water from an urn and returned, placing the bowl in his lap. He wet the cloth thoroughly and took up Jack's hand, wiping away the black of dirt and ash and crusted red from the wounds.

Although it wasn't what Jack expected, he let Lan'do clean first one hand, then the other. The young man rinsed the cloth many times, wiping until he nodded in satisfaction. Then he wet the cloth again and reached to wipe at Jack's flushed face, cleansing his brow of sweat.

Jack sighed and let his eyes fall shut as the cool cloth moved over his skin. Lan'do had a soft touch – the spacer figured he must be a healer of some sort and wasn't that lucky for him? He reopened his eyes when the cloth moved away and he focused on a piece of fruit in front of his lips. Without thinking, he opened his mouth, and Lan'do deftly dropped the moist bite on his tongue.

Lan'do continued to feed him for some time, occasionally having a bite himself. Eventually he set the bowl aside, noting Jack squirming uncomfortably with a knowing smile. Standing, he pointed to the corner of the room where a woven screen stood. Jack's bladder had started screaming for attention some time ago, but he hadn't wanted to be rude to Lan'do. He carefully sat up and swung his legs over the edge of the platform. Lan'do stood back but stayed close, watching Jack with concerned eyes.

Taking a deep breath, Jack stood up clumsily, but faltered, finding right away that any weight on his injured leg hurt badly. Without saying a word, Lan'do shifted under his shoulder, providing him support so he could walk to the corner. Patting his shoulder, Lan'do made sure Jack braced himself against the wall before stepping around the screen. Jack shook his head in wonder at the politeness of these people so far. He relieved himself and did his trousers most of the way back up, then limped heavily to the screen where Lan'do appeared silently and slid under his arm again.

He helped Jack back to the pallet and sat next to him, dampening another cloth and starting to wipe down the spacer's body. At first embarrassed, then slightly aroused, Jack endured Lan'do's economical motions, admittedly refreshed afterward.

Finally Lan'do set aside the cloth and ruffled Jack's hair. "Marsha," he murmured soothingly.

"What?" Jack asked, frowning a bit.

The dark-haired man smiled sweetly and folded his hands under his cheek, closing his eyes for a moment. Then he poked the spacer in the chest.

"Oh. Sleep. Right. You told me that one earlier," Jack said weakly as he lay back.

Lan'do nodded and pulled a light sheet over Jack's legs, going back to lightly finger-combing his patient's hair. Feeling comforted, Jack dropped off to sleep.


HE slept the whole night and next day away in the quiet room. That evening, while Jack crossed the room back to the bed from the privy, Arl'ban appeared in the doorway. The spacer stopped and peered at him – he looked so different. Then he realized the native wore no weapons or paint, only light trousers and a sun-bleached robe over his broad shoulders. Arl'ban gestured behind him and Samuel walked into the room.

"Jack, you're looking a little better," Samuel said.

"I thought you were sleeping," Jack said as Lan'do helped him back to the platform.

"Yeah, I crashed out at Arl'ban's. He must be one of the head guys, he's got a huge suite of rooms," Samuel said. He kissed Jack's temple and cheek before sitting at the foot of the platform.

"I slept here and didn't move, but thanks to Lan'do, I knew where you were," Jack said, pointing at the slim man who perched next to him. Samuel shook his head and glanced to where Arl'ban stood at the door, watching. "Well, he knew you were sleeping, he told me," Jack said as he sighed, relaxing back against the layers of blankets.

Samuel raised a hand, palm out, to Lan'do. "Va hahlo, Lan'do," he said.

Lan'do smiled and glanced to Arl'ban, then back to Samuel. "Va hahlo, Sahmwell," he said, raising a hand as well.

Jack chuckled. "Been talking to Arl'ban again, huh?"

"Well, I figure there's more of them than us, we might as well learn the language," Samuel's square face turned serious. "The ship's totally destroyed, Jack. We're not going anywhere."

Jack stared at his best friend. He noticed Lan'do standing and moving to Arl'ban, apparently giving them some privacy, but he didn't look away from Samuel. "Yeah," he rasped. "I know."

"So we might as well make the best of it, yeah?" Samuel said bravely, though his eyes betrayed pained emotion.

Sighing, Jack nodded. "The kids will be fine, Sammy. We left them plenty, well set up."

Samuel sighed, rubbing at his face. "You know, when Polly brought Harry home all those years ago, and then I met you, I never thought something like this would happen."

Jack chuckled. "You're a privateer, Sammy. How could you not think something like this would happen?"

Shrugging, Samuel relaxed a little. "You feed me, dress me and sleep with me, I guess I figured you'd keep me out of trouble, you know?"

"We're alive, aren't we?" Jack said reasonably.

Samuel laughed. "Yeah, there is that."

Jack glanced over to where Arl'ban and Lan'do stood, murmuring. "We're being kind of rude."

Samuel looked over, caught Arl'ban's eye, and gestured the two natives over. "Chimi," he said.

Arl'ban smiled slightly and approached. "Chisa," he corrected.

Samuel's brow furrowed. "Chisa," he repeated.

Jack looked between them. "What are you saying?"

"Well, I kind of thought 'chimi' was come, but apparently it's more like 'come with me', and 'chisa' is 'come here'," Samuel explained.

Jack looked to see Lan'do still waiting at the door. "Lan'do, chisa," he said. The native smiled and walked over, sitting again on the edge of the platform. "Yeah, I'd say you're right about that."

Arl'ban watched the two strangers for a bit and then spoke at length to Lan'do, who at first seemed surprised. Then he glanced between Samuel and Jack before visibly wilting a bit and nodding. Arl'ban folded his arms and fell silent.

"I wonder what that was about," Jack murmured. Samuel shrugged, looking at the stoic Arl'ban for a clue not forthcoming.

Jack glanced to the disappointed man sitting near him. He reached out to touch him. "Lan'do?" The young man blinked and looked at Jack, his eyes filled with unhappiness the spacer didn't understand. "Lan'do?" he asked again, voice softer.

Lan'do dipped his head and softened his voice. "Sahmwell marshallus a Jahk getana e Jahk risan," he murmured.

"What's that?" Samuel asked, not catching but a few of the words.

Jack held up a hand to silence him. "Lan'do? Samuel marshallus a Arl'ban getana."

Lan'do looked up, confused. He looked to Arl'ban, who shrugged. "Sahmwell marshallus a Jahk getana," Lan'do repeated.

"Jack?" Samuel asked, quieter.

"Something about where you're sleeping," Jack said. "Apparently either in Arl'ban's rooms or here with me, I think."

Samuel frowned, but held his tongue. Jack tried again. "Lan'do? Risan?" he asked, trying to get more information.

Lan'do looked up at him, dark eyes conflicted, and then patted his hand on the soft covers over the platform. "Risan," he whispered.

"Oh. Oh! Ah, Samuel, I think Arl'ban is saying you should sleep here in my room and in my bed," Jack explained. "And apparently Lan'do's not too happy about it."

Samuel chuckled. "Charmed another one, did you? I don't know what it is about you, but hell..." he shook his head in mock disgust. "I fell for you once upon a time. With that face, how do you manage it?"

"Give me a break. So what do you want to do? Stay here with me or stay with Arl'ban?" Jack asked. "Honestly, I think we're pretty safe either way."

"Well, nothing against you, lover boy, but Arl'ban's got several beds and couches, all of which are more comfortable than this thing," Samuel thumped his knuckles on the platform.

Jack chuckled. "You are so spoiled." Samuel grinned in reply and nodded. Jack's brighter blue eyes twinkled. "Shall I explain that you'll sleep in Arl'ban's rooms but not his bed?"

Back straightening in a bit of panic, Samuel glanced to Arl'ban and back to Jack. "Ah... Well..." and he flushed. Jack snickered, and Samuel frowned heavily as his cheeks flushed. "Well, are you going to tell Lan'do that you're happy to sleep in his bed?"

Laughing aloud, Jack laid his hand over Lan'do's to get his attention. "Lan'do, Samuel marshallus a Arl'ban getana, dran Jack risan."

Lan'do perked up and looked over to Arl'ban, who appeared surprised. The warrior shrugged as he glanced to Samuel.

The spacer sighed. "Samuel marshallus a Arl'ban getana," he stated, repeating Jack's words.

"I marshalln a Arl'ban getana," the warrior rumbled.

Samuel rolled his eyes. "Now we're getting grammar lessons."

Jack chuckled. "I marshalln a ...?" he glanced to Lan'do, then around the room.

Lan'do smiled. "Jahk marshallus a Lan'do getana e Jahk risan," he said. Arl'ban snorted quietly, making Samuel snicker.

Jack narrowed his eyes. "What?"

"Arl'ban seems to think that's pretty funny. You sleeping in Lan'do's rooms in your own bed," Samuel said, poking fun.

"We have no idea what they mean by whose bed," Jack defended. "They could just mean ownership. There's nothing sexual about it."

Samuel sighed and stood. "Uh huh. You just remember that when Lan'do's big puppy dog eyes turn on you. Take it easy, Jacky. I'm going to get some food and some sleep."

"Good night, Samuel," Jack waved his hand. "Sleep well in Arl'ban's bed."

Samuel stuck his tongue out at Jack and followed the warrior back out of the room, leaving his laughing friend and a smiling Lan'do behind.

Jack looked back to Lan'do, who watched him with a smile. "I marshalln?" the spacer asked.

Lan'do nodded. "Tarn?" he asked, gesturing about the room. "A iy getana?" He pressed his hand to his chest.

Taking a chance, Jack drew a steady breath. "A Lan'do getana," he replied.

The pleased smile on Lan'do's face proved Jack right. The slim man helped him stand and walk around the corner, down the hall and into a large suite of rooms.

Too tired to look around much, Jack collapsed happily on some sort of sleeping couch near the fire pit. "Simi san," he murmured.

"Va hahlo san," Lan'do said quietly, pulling a light drape over him. "Marsha." The spacer drifted to sleep almost immediately under Lan'do's watchful eyes.

Not too long later, Jack thrashed in a nightmare, waking with a strangled gasp. He felt hands on his shoulders.

"Jahk?"

He opened his eyes, seeing easily in the dim darkness. Lan'do leaned over his pallet, holding his shoulders, looking very worried. Jack gulped for a breath. "I'm okay," he said shakily.

Sinking to perch on the edge of the couch, Lan'do raised an eyebrow in patent disbelief.

Jack sighed. "I can tell you, but you're not going to understand. I was dreaming about the pirates and the attack on the ship... I thought we were going to die..." The tale tumbled out of him, and Lan'do sat, quietly listening, one hand lightly petting Jack's hair.

Sorrowful blue eyes settled on Lan'do. "I don't think I'll ever get home," Jack said sadly. "Not that it's not beautiful here, and you and your people have been great so far..." he trailed off with a sigh, taking some comfort from the fingers ruffling his hair.

Lan'do spoke quietly. "Jahk sullarn auf landa."

Peering up at the other man, Jack slowly shook his head, not understanding.

Standing, Lan'do offered a hand. "Chimi," he invited.

Jack took his hand, and the native helped him to his feet. They crossed the room to the far wall, where Jack could make out drawings. "What is this?" he asked.

Making sure Jack was balanced while propped against the wall, Lan'do fetched a torch and brought it close, illuminating the exquisite art on the stone.

Jack gasped at the detail, the skill evident in the drawings. "Did you do this?" he asked, pointing at Lan'do, then at the wall.

Lan'do nodded. He pointed at a depiction of the tall stone pyramid with a figure near the top, arms raised to the blazing sun above. "Lan'do," he said, first touching the figure, then the sun. "E landa."

"You're named for the sun. You're some sort of priest, aren't you?" Jack murmured.

The slim man moved his arm slightly, lighting more of the picture. Jack's eyes widened as he saw a black streak arching down from the sun over the city, disappearing into the jungle.

"Jahk sullarn auf landa," the native repeated, his finger trailing along the black line in the sky.

"I fell from the sun," Jack whispered. Then he chuckled and nodded. "Well, yeah, I guess that's about right."

"Aye?"

"Aye," Jack agreed, nodding, also tracing the black streak and tapping where it disappeared into the jungle.

Lan'do moved his hand over the city drawn within the jungle. "Lan'do'tay," he said.

"Sun City. That's pretty straightforward," Jack murmured.

The native took the torch back to its sconce before returning to assist Jack back to the sleeping couch, helping him settle and covering him.

Jack grasped Lan'do's arm. "Will you stay here? With me?" he asked, knowing he wasn't communicating well. Lan'do smiled patiently and waited for Jack to rephrase what he said. Nervously, Jack patted his arm. "Lan'do marshallus a Jack risan?"

The other man's lips twitched, so Jack figured he must have mangled the grammar, but he knew he got his point across when Lan'do patted his hip to have him scoot over. The slim man curled up next to him, away from his injured leg, and pillowed his head on Jack's shoulder.

"Marsha," Lan'do said firmly.

Feeling comforted by the warmth next to him, Jack's eyes fell closed.

AFTER leaving Jack in Lan'do's care, Samuel followed Arl'ban through the stone corridor back they way they came, soon re-entering the warrior's rooms. Pausing by a large table, Samuel poured himself a cup of water. "Arl'ban?" he asked, getting the other man's attention. He mimed putting food in his mouth.

"Ah, prang. Dalo." Arl'ban walked back out of the room. Samuel didn't know what he'd said, but felt safe in assuming it was a request to wait. He moved and sat next to the fire pit, shaking his head in wonder at all that had happened in the last two days.

Arl'ban interrupted his musing by re-entering, a slim woman with dark hair and fine features following him carrying a basket. She set it on the table and half bowed. "Simi san, O'lia," Arl'ban said. She smiled and peered curiously at Samuel before she left. "Sahmwell, chisa prangn," the warrior called.

Standing and walking back to the table, Samuel intuitively answered the call to eat and looked into the basket. It held what looked to be flatbread, some dried meat, round fruit and a crock of something creamy. He glanced up at Arl'ban and smiled.

Arl'ban gestured to the food, taking a piece of flatbread himself and pulling the crock out of the basket, dipping the bread in it. Samuel watched and took a piece of bread, dipping the edge in the crock and cautiously tasting the white sauce.

The sauce tasted surprisingly tangy, made with fresh herbs. It reminded him of yogurt. He dipped the bread in the crock liberally, and then wrapped a piece of dried meat in the bread, making a sort of wrap. He moaned happily when he bit into it, drawing a chuckle from Arl'ban.

Samuel narrowed his eyes and frowned at Arl'ban, which only made the other man laugh more. "What?" Samuel asked. "I'm hungry!"

"Huhn-gray." Arl'ban chuckled and mimicked rubbing his stomach, making pleasurable noises before laughing again, those white teeth a contrast against his sun-darkened skin.

"Yeah, you're a funny guy, Arl'ban," Samuel muttered, reaching into the basket for a fruit, which he threw at the other man.

Snickering, Arl'ban caught the fruit and started peeling it. "Frescha?" he asked, eyes still twinkling.

Figuring that could mean many things, Samuel frowned again. "Huh?"

Arl'ban smirked and rubbed his belly again. "Frescha," he drew out, making those pleasurable noises again.

Samuel swallowed hard on the desire that rose in his gut. "Ah, yeah, frescha," he repeated, nodding.

"Aye," the native said, nodding.

Assuming that meant yes, Samuel kept nodding. "Aye, frescha."

Arl'ban nodded and moved from his seat. "San van tahla?"

"Aye, simi san," Samuel answered absently, fixing another wrap. A cup of water soon appeared at his elbow and Arl'ban sat back down with one of his own. They ate in companionable silence until Samuel sat back after his fifth wrap, hugging his stomach. "Frescha," he groaned happily.

Arl'ban chuckled, eyes dancing. "I calln san dran quallo a risan."

When Samuel raised an eyebrow in question, Arl'ban wrapped his arms around his midsection, made a terrible face, bent over and made a noise like vomiting.

Samuel broke out laughing. "No. Dran. Dran quallo?"

Arl'ban, still laughing, nodded. "Dran quallo."

Samuel chuckled and glanced around the room, rubbing his eyes and yawning. "I marshalln?" he asked, hoping Arl'ban would know what he meant.

The warrior nodded and waved a hand, shrugging. Samuel took that to mean he could sleep wherever he wanted. "Simi san," he said, missing Arl'ban's slow nod and intense gaze as the spacer walked over to a long couch with no sides about as big as a bunk on the shuttle and lay down. Arl'ban stood and moved around the room, dousing the torches until only the fire pit lit the room dimly. He laid down on another of the sleeping couches several feet away, watching Samuel sleep for a long time before his own eyes closed.

JACK stood on the balcony, braced on a cane, looking out of the pyramid down onto the grounds. Samuel stood with Arl'ban and a group of other natives. They were apparently discussing training him to use a weapon of some sort. Jack chuckled as Samuel declined the spear taller than himself.

"Jahk?"

The spacer turned to smile at Lan'do. The younger man had been his constant companion for a few weeks now, although he seemed very intuitive and gave Jack space and time alone as well. The spacer spent almost all his time with the beautiful young man, learning about the city and how they lived there, watching Lan'do conduct worship at high noon, swimming in a river nearby, visiting one of the small schools where children played.

Jack felt like he was settling into a new life. He knew many of the natives by name now, and they encouraged him to speak with them. He still spoke half in words and half in gestures, but Jack learned more vocabulary every day. "Hello, Lan'do," he answered in the new language.

"Are you well today?" Lan'do asked politely, standing next to him and looking out over the grounds.

"Yes, I slept well," Jack answered, the foreign words coming easier each time he used them. "And you?"

"I am well," Lan'do replied, smiling genuinely. "What does Sahmwell do?" he asked, looking down from the balcony.

Jack chuckled and leaned slightly on the balcony wall. "Arl'ban teaches Samuel, I think."

Lan'do smiled wider. "Arl'ban is first warrior; he is good," he said with a nod. "Does Sahmwell learn good?"

Jack nodded. "Yes," he murmured, watching Arl'ban place a long dagger in Samuel's hand, almost a short sword, really. "Samuel is a tasty man."

Lan'do laughed. "Sahmwell is a good man," he corrected, eyes dancing.

Flushing, Jack repeated "frecha" as opposed to "frescha".

Grinning, Lan'do nodded. "You are a good man, Jahk," he said, patting the spacer's shoulder.

Swallowing hard as he felt desire for Lan'do bubble inside him, Jack gazed at the other man's profile. His body urged him toward the beautiful young man, but he had no idea about the proprieties concerning it — what if they didn't allow same-sex relations in their culture? It could be a devastating realization. But the tender caring Lan'do bestowed upon him freely had snared Jack's heart and Jack could see himself being very happy here with Lan'do for the rest of their lives.

"Jahk?"

Lan'do's soft voice caught his attention again, and he looked up to see the native studying him, eyes inquisitive. Before Jack could apologize, Lan'do moved close and hugged him carefully. Jack blinked in surprise, but didn't move away, instead savoring the feel of the lean man against him.

"I am happy you are here, Jahk," Lan'do whispered before kissing his cheek and stepping back smiling and leaving the balcony. Jack watched him go, stunned, and thought maybe he might have a little better idea about the proprieties now. With a sigh he looked down into the courtyard in time to see Samuel waving at him. He raised a hand in salute and hobbled inside to sit back down and spend some time thinking.

Outside, Samuel attacked a wooden pole with a long, dulled knife, receiving guidance from Arl'ban and another warrior. When Arl'ban called a halt to all the practice in the courtyard, he patted the spacer on the shoulder and indicated he should sit on a bench to the side. Samuel did so as he watched a few older men take seats as well, carrying what looked like large, long flutes.

The warriors mingled, teasing and laughing while the flutes began to play a slow, measured melody. The men started to fall into rough lines, moving in precise, unhurried gestures, almost like a choreographed dance. Samuel watched, fascinated, as more and more joined in, floating as one to the flowing music blown from wooden reeds. Legs went from stiff to fluid, hands from fisted to flat-palmed, all in time, all in unison.

He saw a few children around the edges, trying to mimic the movements. The warriors smiled and merely shifted around them when need be, sometimes reaching out to correct a form. After a few minutes, the dance stilled and then started again from the beginning.

Samuel looked through the lines until he found Arl'ban. Rather than standing at the lead, he moved in a random line, his eyes closed as his body flowed with the music. Balance and grace in such a honed and muscled body made for an incredible sight. Arl'ban stretched as the others did, the expanse of bared skin warmed in the sunlight, and Samuel felt the pull of want in his gut that seemed to grow with each passing day. Partway through the form, some of the women nearby began to sing in counterpoint, enriching the atmosphere. The dance went on through several cycles before stopping, and the spacer remained entranced by Arl'ban the entire time. Samuel was still watching him when the warrior opened his eyes. Arl'ban's lips quirked self-deprecatingly, and warriors speaking to him drew his attention away.

Waiting, Samuel wondered how long it would take him to learn such a dance. While it didn't look exceedingly difficult, he knew it surely couldn't be all that simple.

"It was good?"

Samuel looked up to see Arl'ban towering over him. "Yes. Good, good," he answered, scooting over on the bench so the native could sit next to him. "I learn?"

Arl'ban looked surprised but pleased. "Yes, as you want."

Nodding, Samuel leaned back against the stone wall. "I want. It is..." he shook his head, not knowing a word. Arl'ban nodded, understanding.

That evening, Lan'do and Jack walked through the halls to a larger room filled with small tables, low to the ground, for their evening meal. Many men and women sat in the room eating, and several raised hands in greeting to Lan'do and the spacer.

Jack stopped at a table in one corner where Arl'ban and Samuel sat waiting, laughing about something. "What is funny?" he asked good-naturedly.

Arl'ban snickered. "Sahmwell."

Samuel rolled his eyes. "I made a fool of myself with the knife today, and Arl'ban thinks it's hysterical," he said.

Jack thumped Samuel on the shoulder, as he did whenever his friend lapsed into their former language. Samuel huffed. "I learn no good," he said in their adopted language.

Arl'ban snickered again. The tall, stoic man had loosened up quite a bit over the last few weeks. Jack suspected being around Samuel made the difference. He'd seen Arl'ban watching his friend closely with a wistful look in his eyes before hiding it. Jack chuckled and glanced to Samuel, who crossed his arms and affected a petulant face.

"Be kind, Arl'ban, few are good as you," Lan'do scolded lightly. Arl'ban's lips twisted in amusement, but he stopped laughing and nodded.

"No kind and no good," Samuel muttered good-naturedly as he pulled apart his piece of flatbread. Jack snorted.

After eating, Jack looked over to Samuel, noting the tired lines of his face. "Are you sleeping, Samuel?" he asked before switching languages. "You don't look like you feel well."

Samuel blinked out of his daze and smiled tiredly. "Arl'ban's a hard teacher," he answered so the other men would understand as he glanced to the one he spoke of. "I'm just tired. Simi san."

Jack nodded. "You are welcome," he murmured, gaining an inquisitive look from Lan'do. His dark eyes reflected concern.

Arl'ban watched Samuel closely, eyes narrowing as he stopped eating. "Come with me, Sahmwell," he invited, standing from the table. "San marshallus."

Samuel smiled and clapped Jack's shoulder. "I sleep," he said.

"Sleep good." Jack echoed his goodbye in their adopted language.

Dinner passed quietly, and afterward Jack lay on a couch and watched Lan'do draw on the wall. It appeared to be a depiction of the warriors practicing in the courtyard, with one conspicuously taller blond man in their midst. Jack smiled.

"Samuel no like fight," he offered.

Lan'do nodded. "To fight is no good," he said, tucking dark curls behind his ear. "But fight we must."

Jack watched Lan'do move sinuously, a terribly appealing unconscious motion. The spacer shifted uncomfortably as his body reacted. "I walk, Lan'do," Jack said finally. The priest nodded, distracted, and Jack escaped.

He returned to the smaller rooms assigned to him. He rarely went there, but he wouldn't be disturbed as he dealt with his attraction toward Lan'do. Jack sprawled on the pallet, one hand clutching himself and rubbing until he curled on his side, gasping as the heat contracted and coiled inside him, breaking free in several pulses of come as he breathed Lan'do's name.

IN an attempt to make a clean break with the past, Samuel and Jack decided to make a trip to the wrecked ship to salvage anything they might want to keep – personal possessions, mostly. First Aid materials, perhaps some emergency rations and flares – anything usable after a month of exposure to the humid jungle.

Arl'ban argued against their decision to return to the ship. He tried to explain about the dangers of the jungle, but Lan'do finally told him to be quiet and allow the two spacers do as they wished. Jack figured the priest knew the two men needed closure. Arl'ban answered by leading a scouting party to escort them. Then Lan'do decided he wanted to go along too, so it became a long day's hike in good company. They would take their time and sleep once each way, since there was no reason to hurry.

Jack didn't mind. He could talk with Lan'do, work on learning more words. And he knew Samuel wouldn't mind Arl'ban around, either.

They were sitting around small camp fires that night, talking quietly as some men slept, when a ruckus in the jungle stirred the warriors to awareness. When a cry of warning echoed through the vegetation, Arl'ban hissed and grabbed his spear.

Before Samuel or Jack could react, grayed shadows slipped out the dark, almost invisible, rushing in to attack.

"Go!" Arl'ban ordered after knocking one of the aggressors to the ground with a heavy fist. "Go and be safe, Sahmwell." He pointed as two more dark fighters attacked him.

Jack looked for Lan'do, but couldn't find him amongst the grappling warriors who fought throughout the ruined camp. He stepped slowly backward, trying to locate him, worried. He knew Lan'do would not fight.

When Arl'ban kicked an enemy into one of the fires, the two spacers started to move as they listened to the man's shrieks. But Samuel fought running away.

"We've got to help Arl'ban! We can go back!"

"We'd just worry him, Sammy. Come on! The best thing we can do is get to the ship where Arl'ban and Lan'do can find us."

So they stumbled through the jungle into the night.


SAMUEL crouched by the bubbling river, soaking the shirt in his hands, then beating it against a rock before wetting it again and wringing it out. He peered across the light rapids to where Jack climbed up the rock waterfall. Smiling, Samuel shaded his eyes and watched his friend's ascent. Once attaining the top, Jack pulled fruit off the highest tree branches and tossed it into the still pool that eddied to the side of the falls.

Watching the round, peach-colored fruit float, Samuel thought about the last two days in the jungle. Oddly enough, he felt content, though he keenly longed for Arl'ban and all the warmth associated with his friend and teacher – and perhaps someday lover. Samuel didn't miss the cold of space as he'd once feared he would, and he knew Jack felt the same. They both now took some comfort from the humid surrounds that evoked

Lan'do'tay. Surely Arl'ban was not far away, he knew where to find the wrecked vessel. But the unknown of that distance bothered Samuel. He felt unaccountably adrift even with Jack here.

Jack stood atop the waterfall, feet in the splashing water, looking down to where they'd camped last night. Raising his chin, he looked out over the jungle, straining to make out any large structures that might hint at the temple. They'd hiked far enough down the mountain that he couldn't see the structure that dominated Lan'do'tay, but he could easily make out the trench carved into the earth from their crash landing a few weeks ago. That meant they were getting closer. He didn't really remember how long it had taken them to get to Sun City the first time.

Jack snorted. In the two days, he and Samuel had seen no animal larger than a monkey. But they heard the larger animals moving around, hidden in the shadows, and they remained cautious and alert as they traveled through the virgin landscape. Jack hoped it was a case of "don't bother us; we won't bother you." Stretching in the sunlight, the spacer felt the warmth soak into his skin and muscles — much more developed now than a month ago. Jack smirked. They both felt quite at home, adapting to living in the jungle, helping forage for food and avoiding natural hazards, even learning to sleep in the trees comfortably. However, neither of them could cook. Hence, the fruit his climb had yielded. Jack looked down the thirty-foot falls and waved at Samuel, who raised a hand in return, shading his eyes from the bright sunlight.

Samuel chuckled and shook his head ruefully as Jack mimed diving off the falls. His longtime friend had discovered a rugged streak that gave the blond spacer no end of amusement. They'd both slimmed down and developed more musculature, he realized, shaking his head as he looked down at himself. Still stocky, still broad, but more defined.

"I look like a warrior," Samuel murmured to himself in his old language, smiling. "Arl'ban's really whipped me into shape."

"*You need work,*" Arl'ban said.

"*Work?*" Samuel asked as they walked toward the courtyard pool after practicing with the warriors.

"*Yes,*" the native said, poking Samuel's arm. "Skeewah."

"*That doesn't sound good,*" Samuel muttered to himself, hoping he would pick up more of the new language soon. "Skeewah?" he repeated, questioning.

*Stopping in front of the water, Arl'ban nodded. He pulled up his arm, flexing, showing off an impressive muscle.* "Vorlash," *he said, pointing to it.* "Skeewah." *He poked at the blond's arm again.*

*Samuel's jaw dropped in amused indignation.* "Skinny? You're calling me skinny? Me?" *He was easily one of the largest men in the city. He poked back at Arl'ban's arm, noticing his eyes dancing in amusement.* "Oh, you're a funny guy, Arl'ban. Arl'ban is funny."

"Sken-nee," *Arl'ban chuckled, poking again at Samuel's arm.*

*Hoping to catch the warrior off guard, Samuel rushed at him and succeeded in toppling him backward into the pool. Arl'ban came up spluttering, peering at Samuel in disbelief from under dripping hair.*

"Skeewah." *Samuel drawled the new word as he pointed at Arl'ban, grinning and leaning on the edge of the pool.*

*What a mistake.*

*Pushing up with the strength of his legs, Arl'ban rose out of the water in a rush and grabbed him, dragging Samuel into the pool before the spacer could so much as yelp. They played in the water, splashing each other for some time before companionably heading back to the temple for some dinner. But Samuel looked his fill of Arl'ban's muscular body draped in wet cloth, and when Arl'ban worked outside that evening, he thought about the warrior while stroking himself to a quiet orgasm.*

"Hey, Sammy?"

Blinking, Samuel pulled himself out of memory. "Yeah, Jack?" he asked, turning his chin to see his friend nearby, having descended the falls when he wasn't paying attention.

"I'm glad I didn't slip and break something, I had to call your name three times," Jack said with a smile, crouching next to his friend.

Samuel smiled ruefully, cheeks a bit flushed. "Just thinking about the day Arl'ban called me skinny." He glanced down at his ripped chest and abs. "Skeewah. Only now I'm more vorlash."

Jack nodded. "Yeah, I know what you mean." He flexed his arm, moderately impressed with himself.

"What does Lan'do think about you being all muscle-bound?" Samuel asked, leaning back on his elbows. "He's a smaller guy."

"Smaller compared to Arl'ban, yeah, but he's pretty fit himself," Jack said, sitting down and propping his arms on his knees, remembering.

*"Come, Jahk, we walk," Lan'do said.*

*"Where?" Jack asked, taking his cane and following at a hobble.*

*"We walk, Jahk," the dark-haired man said with a smile, beckoning for him to follow. And walk they did, from building to building, visiting the elderly and the children, caring for the sick, helping with chores. Jack was exhausted halfway through the day, whereas Lan'do continued on, tireless.*

*A woman offered Jack a cup of water, which he gratefully accepted as he sat down. Her body shone tanned and golden, and her blond hair tumbled over one shoulder as she smiled shyly at him. She had a sweet face. Lan'do patted her shoulder. "This is Ina'lan'da," he said.*

*"Woman of the sun. Yes, I see," Jack said with a smile, pointing to her hair, unusual in the tribe. He and Samuel were such a curiosity for just that reason, their light coloring and hair, not to mention Jack's bright blue eyes, which fascinated the natives.*

*She nodded, only to be distracted by a small child patting her knee. She lifted the boy to her lap. "Tseh'tah'la," she said, patting the child's hair.*

*"Your boy?" Jack asked.*

*Ina'lan'da nodded. "You have boy?" she asked slowly, so he could understand.*

*Jack nodded. "Harry. He is big," he answered.*

*"Ah, good," Ina'lan'da said with a smile. "Boy good."*

*"Lacaum good," Lan'do said fondly.*

*"Yes, lacaum," she agreed. "Tseh'tah'la is boy of Lan'do."*

*Jack's brows flew up, and he looked to the priest, who flushed in embarrassment. "Boy of Lan'do?" he asked, half amused, half worried. Was this Lan'do's wife? Only then a warrior entered the house and greeted Ina'lan'da with a loving kiss, taking the boy in his arms and swinging the giggling child around. Lan'do gestured for Jack to join him, and they left the happy family.*

*"Boy of Lan'do?" Jack asked again, this time not quite as worried.*

*The priest still looked embarrassed. "They had no lacaum," he tried to explain.*

*"Lacaum?" Jack asked. The priest pointed to the children who ran by, playing tag. "Oh, they had no children." Lan'do looked*

*relieved and nodded. Jack chuckled and nudged the priest's arm, getting another flush and rueful smile as they walked along.*

"We know more of the language now," Samuel said, breaking Jack from his reverie. "It's only been four weeks and I understand Arl'ban and O'lia a lot better. What about you?"

The other man nodded as the pleasant memory faded. "I can hear it sometimes, when I dream, and I understand. I think in it and speak it later," Jack said. He grinned. "I guess that means we're settling in."

Samuel chuckled, and they sat quietly beside the rapids, watching the water spill over the rocks before they went back to their hike toward the ship.

The vessel looked pretty much as they'd left it. The two men found some evidence of animals inside the craft and water damage, but otherwise it appeared untouched. They spent a couple of days salvaging what they could – clothing, stored rations, First Aid kits, even a portable viewer and several photo cartridges. If the entire party had been here, it would have taken only a matter of hours. Packing the goods into satchels, they sat outside on the wing, much like that first time when they met the natives. Samuel let his eyes go out of focus as he remembered.

*"What is this?" Arl'ban asked, pointing to the First Aid kit Samuel brought with him from the crash site.*

*"It is for sick," Samuel strung together with his nearly nonexistent vocabulary.*

*"Sick?" Arl'ban tapped the closed box, tilting his head as he studied it. He ran his fingers over the seals, puzzling it out and opening it without Samuel's help. "Ah, hearteno tseh Lan'do," he said.*

*"Harr-teeno?" Samuel repeated.*

*Arl'ban frowned slightly, trying to translate. "Sick. Lan'do, hearteno, no sick." He plucked the bandages from the kit and gestured with them.*

*"Hearteno is a healer, then," Samuel concluded. "Lan'do hearten?"*

*"Lan'do hearteus," Arl'ban corrected mildly, poking through the kit some more, shaking his head when he didn't recognize anything else. He spouted a bunch of words Samuel couldn't follow and closed the kit.*

"What's up, Samuel?" Jack finally asked. "You're quiet."

Samuel shrugged, blinking away the memory, squatting next to his pack. "I guess I figured he'd be here," he said with a slight smile. "Obviously he was upset when he sent us on, to get us away from those men. I hope everyone is okay."

Jack understood immediately. "I'm sure he's fine, Sammy," he murmured. "Arl'ban's the best, right?"

"Yeah, he is," the other man replied, eyes faraway.

Leaning over to nudge Samuel's shoulder, Jack waggled his eyebrows with a grin. "What else is he the best at?"

Samuel flushed dark red and Jack laughed. "Bastard," Samuel muttered.

"Heh. Is that how it is then? Are you lovers?" Jack prodded.

"Lov... No!" Samuel answered in shock. "I don't even know if they go for that kind of thing here. I wouldn't want to insult him. He could bend me into a pretzel."

"Hmmm. Yeah. Useful, that," Jack said with a dreamy smile.

Samuel thumped Jack's chest. "Hey, keep your thoughts on your dark-eyed priest, bud," he warned.

Jack grinned. Lan'do was a gorgeous man. "Yeah, yeah. Fine. Live in denial. Go ahead."

Samuel snorted. "I'm not denying that I want Arl'ban. I just don't know what to do about it. Ask him to go to bed with me, I guess."

"As good a place to start as any," Jack agreed, not mentioning that he'd slept in Lan'do's bed from that first night. Chastely. It drove him crazy when he woke up aroused and alone each morning. He stood up and stretched, rubbing his eyes before leaning over and nudging Samuel. "You were the one paying attention that day. What direction do we go?" Jack asked with a crooked smile. "Not that I'm worried. We're supposed to be only a day's hard hike from the city, but if we get lost, it could take a lot longer."

Samuel nodded. "That way," he said as he pointed.

They shouldered the packs and departed the sunny clearing, following Samuel's memory into the shadows. As the terrain became steeper, both men fashioned stout walking sticks, helpful for balancing on the hillsides and rough paths that curled through the brush. They talked as they walked along. Samuel admitted late that night that he thought they should have been at Lan'do'tay by now, but Jack shook his head and laughed. They couldn't be far, but the small mountains would make it impossible to see the temple until they practically stumbled over it.

"Arl'ban will never let me forget this," Samuel muttered.

Jack chuckled. "Me either, Oh Master Navigator." The other man smacked him on the arm, and they kept walking.

Tired, they found a thick-bodied tree to climb and rest in, feeling more secure off the jungle floor where animals roamed at night. Samuel had slept with a snake the first night of their journey. The next morning he woke with it curled up against his belly for warmth. Jack still laughed when he remembered the look of pure disbelief on his friend's face. Luckily, the good-natured snake had merely slithered off into the brush.

They settled into the pressing darkness, extinguishing their phosphorus lamps, trying to get comfortable, Samuel on perfunctory watch. Jack dozed peaceably until his friend's hiss woke him.

"Samuel?" he asked sleepily.

"Jacky, wake up, Jacky. Something's about," Samuel warned in a low, serious voice.

An icy tendril of healthy fear woke Jack quickly. In the past days, they'd enjoyed incredibly good luck, avoiding the predators of the jungle so far. As he focused on listening to the jungle around them, eyes closed, he agreed. It was far too quiet.

The attack came suddenly, and neither of them had a chance to react.

Before Samuel could move, a heavy, warm, furry bulk struck him full in the chest, fire erupting down his side as he felt claws score him. With a wild scream, he fought back, kicking and punching the shadow draped over him.

Jack tensed as the big cat's cry nearly deafened him and he recoiled as the shadow, darker than the jungle around them, flew past him, pouncing into the tree where Samuel perched above. Shocked, Jack peered up into the dark, rustling leaves, helpless.

Overwhelmed by the cat's body, Samuel knew he was still alive because he was so much smaller than the animal, which made it even more terrifying; the cat must have been seven feet long. He tucked his head closer against the cat's body and held on. He didn't want that huge mouth of teeth he could feel huffing hot breath above him getting any closer. His heel slid off the thick branch, and Samuel reacted without thinking, sliding away from the fumbling cat's body and off the branch, literally throwing himself from the tree.

"Sammy!" Jack screamed as he saw the other man fall past him, pitching into the darkness and brush below, landing with a sickening thud. Although he first thought to jump down after him, he froze against the tree trunk as he heard the feral growl and pacing above him.

Then the cat sprang for the ground.

"Sammy!" Jack yelled again, hoping his friend could avoid the black-furred predator. He could see some, his eyes having adjusted to the dark, but he knew the cat's eyes were much better.

By luck, Samuel actually landed on his side, keeping his breath, and the smaller branches broke enough of his momentum to leave him only slightly stunned. He drew a breath and moved, stumbling to his feet and crashing through the brush. He needed to get away, and then up out of sight again, hopefully before the cat could track him, he thought clearly. But the blood from the cat's claws and branches was a problem.

Somehow he found a path through the brush and was able to move at a fair clip, but then he heard Jack yell again and something crashing through the brush. The blond spacer hoped like hell that meant the cat was chasing him instead of mauling his friend. Gritting his teeth against the pain, he ran faster, the weeks of life in Lan'do'tay having honed his body.

Ducking instinctively as he heard the cat screeching and prowling through the brush, he narrowly avoided the predator's pounce, smiling grimly as he heard a frustrated growl after the cat slammed into a tree rather than its prey. He left the path at a sharp angle, skidding down an embankment, hoping to find a tree to climb, hoping he could get higher than the much-larger cat.

But his luck ran out.

Gasping for breath, Samuel stopped against a cliff wall, blind, looking back up from where he came and seeing the cat prowling at the top of the hill. He smashed his back against the wall, breathing harshly, clutching his side. He was well and truly trapped. He heard his name echo through the jungle, not too far away, but far enough. Jack would not arrive in time, even if he could stop the predator that now advanced on Samuel slowly, yellow eyes glittering.

The huge black-furred animal crept down the hill with a careful slink, its prey in sight, a long, pink tongue extending from its ash gray maw. Samuel closed his eyes for a moment, sending a goodbye to Polly, his daughter, Jack, his best friend ... and Arl'ban, his quiet warrior and possibly newfound love... before opening them to focus on the means of his end. Time slowed as he watched the cat curl back on its hind legs to spring. His panting echoed harshly in his ears as he shuddered, gritting his teeth, determined to face the animal. With a shrieking cry, the panther launched itself at Samuel, claws and teeth splayed.

Between the thumps of his heart, Samuel saw the cat jump, but out of nowhere a long, muscled body slammed into its soft belly with an enraged howl, knocking the predator to the side. As the spacer gasped in shock and near-hysterical relief, a figure rolled with the animal, grappling with it, the flash of a knife catching the low light as the animal scrambled for purchase by digging long claws into the man's body, trying to escape. In another handful of heartbeats they rolled and the man pinned the cat down and slashed at its throat, then slammed his fists down on its neck, breaking its spine. The cat's dying scream echoed off the stone.

It was over in seconds.

Half bent, arm wrapped to press his hand against his injured side, Samuel stepped away from the cliff wall toward the man who stood over the cat's body in the suffocating shadows. "Telle?" the spacer rasped, saying hello tentatively in the language of Lan'do'tay. It wasn't one of the gray-skinned warriors of the opposing tribe, that much he could tell.

The man turned in the heavy shadows and walked straight to Samuel, closing his arms about the wounded man with one broken groan: "Sahmwell."

Samuel knew immediately who was holding him and he choked out his name in disbelief. "Arl'ban."

The warrior clutched him close. Samuel was shaking after his close call with death, but he could think of nothing better to help him than finding himself in Arl'ban's arms. Samuel recognized that he had fallen hard for the stoic man and he simply couldn't help himself.

"Sahmwell," the tall native pleaded softly, pulling back and cupping the blond man's cheek. "Are you healthy?" Concern was clear on Arl'ban's face.

Samuel's bark of laughter was rueful. "Aye, aye," he said, forgetting all about the scores down his side that were still bleeding lightly. "We've been waiting for you to show up, you big lug," he joked weakly.

Arl'ban's eyes glittered in the dim light and he tilted his head in question, making Samuel realize he hadn't spoken in the native's language.

"Simi san," Samuel settled on, not able to think of any other words in his exhaustion.

Jack stopped at the top of the hill, scrambling to keep his balance as he peered down into the dimly lit area, seeing the two men standing together. "Sammy?" Apprehensive, Jack slid down the slope to come to a stop next to them. "Arl'ban?" He nearly collapsed in relief.

Samuel moved to help his friend get his feet under him. "Jack, are you all right? Did the cat get you?"

Jack shook his head. "I'm fine… Arl'ban?" he asked, surprise clear.

The warrior smiled. "Hello Jahk."

"Hello! My God!" Jack moved to hug the warrior and thump his back. "Sammy, what the hell happened?"

Samuel recounted his nearly tragic encounter with the cat, telling Arl'ban's part. Jack shook his head in wonder, taking in the huge corpse of the animal on the jungle floor, then looked up at Arl'ban and the bloody scores down his back. "You need a healer... both of you do. Arl'ban, is Lan'do here?" Jack asked.

Arl'ban went still, looking at Samuel, and turned a concerned face to the other man. "He is not here."

"He's not here?" Jack echoed. "Where is he?"

Arl'ban looked at Samuel in consternation, then he rambled in his own language, obviously trying to explain. A couple times he pointed at the panther. Both men listened, picking some words out.

"I think he's saying he went... to the what? Into the... dark? With the dark?" Samuel puzzled out.

"The dark? What does that mean?" Jack asked, gut filling with dread. "Does it have something to do with that other tribe that attacked us? The gray-skinned warriors?"

Arl'ban sighed. "Eristahe," he finally said. "Lan'do is not here."

"Arl'ban, eristahe?" Samuel asked.

The proud warrior went down on one knee, folding his hands and holding them up to Samuel. "Eristahe," he said.

The blond man clasped Arl'ban's hands. "He's apologizing."

"Arl'ban, you are a good man," Jack said as he encouraged him to stand, though his worry showed easily.

"Simi san," Arl'ban said seriously, eyes bleak.

"Arl'ban, where is Lan'do'tay?" Samuel asked. They needed to get back to the city.

The native looked around the jungle, getting his bearings, and nodded, taking Samuel by the hand and leading them up the steep hill. Jack followed, his gut clenching. Before long they rejoined a group of Arl'ban's warriors, who all looked equally grim. They took a few minutes as Arl'ban looked over the slashes down Samuel's side and another warrior did the same for him before they started back to the city.

After several hours of hiking, Jack doubted he and Samuel would have found Lan'do'tay without help. When the sun broke the horizon, he looked up through the trees and saw the temple. Wanting to get an explanation from Lan'do, he took off through the brush.

"Jack!" Samuel called, but Arl'ban held his arm to keep him from following. "What, Arl'ban?"

"Lan'do is not here," Arl'ban said, his normally reserved face showing regret. The blond man looked at him for a long moment, then nodded and walked alongside the warrior into the city.

Running ahead, Jack navigated the outskirts of the jungle until he entered the city, surprising a few artisans, but he hurried toward the temple and the man he hoped to find within. "Lan'do!" he yelled as he entered the bottom level, running to the steps that would lead up into the temple.

Turning familiar corners, he skidded to a stop near O'lia, who gaped at him. "O'lia, where is Lan'do?" he asked, his hand gripping her elbow.

She blinked in surprise and shook her head. "Lan'do... Lan'do is not here," she stuttered out before a flood of other words followed that Jack couldn't follow.

Shaking his head, he left her standing in the hall, running to Lan'do's suite. "Lan'do!" he called out as he entered the rooms, out of breath. "Lan'do?"

Jack looked around the chamber — it looked nearly untouched. Shaking his head, he jogged to the empty and still bedchamber. "Lan'do?"

Brow furrowing in disappointment and now worry, Jack turned to see a tall, older man standing in the doorway, dressed in robes similar to what Lan'do wore.

"Lan'do is not here," the older man said kindly, sympathetically.

Jack bowed politely, but his upset could not be hidden. "Please, where is Lan'do?"

The wrinkled and white-haired man gestured for Jack to be seated on one of the pallets around the fire pit and he sat as well, before sighing. "Hello. I am Evas'in." He tapped his chest.

"Hello Evas'in," Jack said quietly, looking over the oldest native he'd seen yet. "I am Jack."

The old priest lowered his eyes, face growing serious. "Lan'do vorasknus a quildaenen."

The spacer shook his head, not understanding. "Vorasknus? Quildaenen?"

Tilting his head, Evas'in held his hand out into the shining sun that broke through the window, then waved his other hand through the shadow cast. "Quildaen." Then he hit one fist in his palm. "Voraskn," he said in a growl.

"Fighting shadows," Jack said, understanding. "I hope Lan'do is well?"

Evas'in slowly shrugged and shook his head. He did not know. He rose and moved to pat Jack on the back. "Sleep," the old priest suggested before leaving silently.

After Jack left, Samuel followed Arl'ban into the temple, surprised when the warrior turned away from the direction of his rooms. "Arl'ban?" he asked, trailing along as the other man led him to a stairway going down under the temple.

"Come with me, Sahmwell," Arl'ban said, holding out a hand at the top of the steps.

Studying him, Samuel looked into the gold-flecked brown eyes, measuring his gaze before nodding and placing his hand in the warrior's. Strong fingers closed around his palm, deceptively soft skin brushing along his. Samuel started slightly at the sparks that jumped from their fingers. At the bottom of the steps, torches flickered to light the way and Arl'ban led him into a humid warmth that reminded Samuel of a sauna. They rounded a corner to stand in front of a stone pool, obviously a cultivated hot spring, shimmered under the firelight. Samuel groaned happily, drawing a chuckle from the warrior. Before, they'd always bathed in the cool pool of water in the courtyard.

Arl'ban trailed his fingers through the water. "Warm," he said.

Dipping his hand, Samuel smiled. "Good," he replied, sitting on the edge of the pool to unlace his boots. Arl'ban walked to the side of the room, returning with a cloth and small pot. He turned Samuel to the side, cleaned the wounds on his ribs, and rubbed in a heavy salve. Once done, Samuel did the same for him, wincing over how deep some of the claw marks where.

Arl'ban took the supplies away and came back with two large cloths Samuel supposed would serve as towels. Then the spacer paused as it struck him that he would be bathing — nude, presumably. Not noticing Samuel's pause, Arl'ban unbuckled his belt, laying it and the dagger aside, the loose trousers easily slipping over his hips to the floor to pool about his feet. In seconds, he wasn't wearing a stitch and Samuel found himself hard pressed not to stare as the muscled legs stepped over the wall and into the water. When swimming in the river or washing in the courtyard, they'd always worn clothes.

"Come here, Sahmwell," Arl'ban invited, patting the top of the water. "Warm," he said.

Swallowing hard, Samuel figured Arl'ban's stripping down meant they didn't have nudity taboos, so he pulled his shirt over his head and shucked his loose pants. He slid into the water, finding it deeper than he expected, and he lifted his eyes to see green ones watching him seriously. "Warm," Samuel murmured.

Arl'ban smiled and leaned back into the water, ducking his head and wetting his hair before lazily swimming across the pool, leaving Samuel to his own devices.

Samuel wondered if that meant Arl'ban's seeming interest simply didn't exist. He sighed, trying to will his erection away. Maybe he ought to go find pretty O'lia... A splash distracted him and Samuel looked up to see Arl'ban pull his long body up onto the edge of the pool before he reached into a basket, bringing back a full cup. Crackling flames from the brazier clearly lit every muscled line of Arl'ban's body, set off by the streaming water. Samuel forced himself to breathe, moving one hand under the water to grip his erection. Desire ate at him.

Watching, mesmerized as the warrior slipped back into the water, he waited as Arl'ban cut through the pool to stop near him, offering the cup.

"What is it?" Samuel asked, a handy phrase he'd learned his first day here.

"For wash," Samuel translated from Arl'ban's answer as the taller man poured some of the oil into his hand and rubbed it on the blond man's chest. His free hand pressed a soft, damp cloth over the cuts in Samuel's side.

Samuel stifled a moan. "Thank you," he murmured, taking the proffered cup.

"You are welcome," Arl'ban answered, tilting his head. "Help?"

Samuel peered at him, confused. Arl'ban reached out to Samuel's shoulders and turned him around, then the spacer gasped as a firm hand slid over his shoulders and down his back, stroking firmly, rubbing the oil into his skin. The spacer relaxed under the massage... and tensed under Arl'ban's touch.

Samuel's eyes fluttered shut as Arl'ban dropped the cloth and moved his hands down the spacer's back and under the water to his waist and hips. Samuel groaned softly as the long fingers moved up his ribs and around to his chest. He hoped very much this meant what he thought it did, and his breathing picked up under Arl'ban's ministrations.

The warrior's hands dipped back under the water, still stroking over his belly, then pausing at his hips. "Sahmwell?" Arl'ban asked quietly, moving close enough that the spacer could feel a column of firm flesh against his hip.

"Yes?" Samuel rasped, afraid to move for fear Arl'ban would stop.

He gasped as Arl'ban pulled him firmly back against his own muscled body, pinning Arl'ban's hardened cock between them. "Are you well?" the warrior asked in a soft tone, hands moving again.

"No," Samuel growled.

"No?" Arl'ban asked, a tinge of concern in his voice.

At the end of his patience, Samuel caught Arl'ban's hands and moved them below the water to cover his aching cock, and his groan echoed over the water as he felt soft lips touch his shoulder. Feeling the strong arms surround him, Samuel relaxed back against Arl'ban.

Full lips trailed along his neck, kissing and nipping, a warm tongue extending to lick along the shell of his ear, dragging a shiver out of Samuel. The long fingers under the water started a firm stroke. "Jemma," Arl'ban breathed against his ear, and the spacer shuddered.

"Oh yes, yes," Samuel moaned, raising one arm behind him to curl it about Arl'ban's neck, his hips shifting to thrust into the fist surrounding his erection. "Please." Arl'ban groaned quietly, shifting his own hips to rut slowly against Samuel's thigh as he caressed his new lover. The warrior's mouth tasted every inch of skin it could reach.

It didn't take long for Samuel to seize with pleasure, his breaths coming hard and fast as he choked out a soft cry, shaking in Arl'ban's arms. The warrior held him close, undulating against him in search of his own completion, and not long after Samuel he hissed, shuddering as he came quietly, his arms tightening around the spacer. After a long moment, the blond man turned enough in Arl'ban's arms to kiss him thoroughly.

When Samuel managed to recover his balance and sense, Arl'ban waited, smirking. He squeezed Samuel's arm. "Skinny," he pronounced.

Samuel huffed an exaggerated sigh and turned fully against Arl'ban's body, his head tilted back to look into his sparkling eyes. "Skinny," he murmured. He stroked over the warrior's muscled shoulders and arms. "Strong..." he drew out throatily.

Arl'ban's breath caught and he closed his arms around his lover, sliding his hands down over Samuel's trim build – "Skinny" – and below the water to the blond man's generous erection. "Strong," the native drew out in a husky hiss.

Pulse hammering, Samuel captured Arl'ban's mouth, the heat between them quickly spiraling again as they grappled, stroking and rubbing wet, heated skin. Samuel wrapped himself around Arl'ban, and his mouth slid over the other man's strong neck until he drew a loud gasp. Grinning, he pulled back to see Arl'ban's eyes dark with desire.

"Sahmwell," Arl'ban growled. "Please." His hands slid to cup Samuel's rear and pull him up against his own re-hardened cock.

"Oh yeah," Samuel muttered, hitching his thigh over Arl'ban's hip. They slowly rutted against each other until their moans and panting filled the room.

Arl'ban's hands moved until his fingers slid into the crease of Samuel's ass. The spacer groaned and pushed back against him. "Please," Samuel whispered into his lover's ear.

Reaching to the side of the pool as he turned Samuel to lean his belly against the stone edge, Arl'ban scooped oil into his hand, coated his fingers, and slid them back into the hot, close crack. He sought the hole there, and one finger sank in slowly, eased by the oil. Before long, taking his cue from Samuel's moans and shivers of pleasure, Arl'ban added a second and then a third, only stopping with his lover began to beg.

Samuel groaned and gasped, fingers clutching the stone until Arl'ban turned him around. "Arl'ban?" he asked, and the warrior stepped close and lifted him to sit on the pool's edge, bringing his body out of the water. Samuel wrapped his legs around Arl'ban's waist. "Please," he asked, extending his chin to reach his lover's mouth and nip at Arl'ban's full, moist lips.

"Yes," Arl'ban groaned as he lined up his swollen erection with his lover's heat and started to rock slowly inward, over and over until Samuel thought he would cry from it. He knew he would never forget this feeling, this overwhelming and loving possession. Arl'ban surged into him, and Samuel's yell of pleasure echoed off the damp stone walls. Pulling Samuel into his arms, Arl'ban held him firmly as he thrust up and in, over and over, driving them crazy and breathless.

"Sahmwell..." Arl'ban called desperately. "Sahmwell..." The loud moan as he exploded inside his lover filled Samuel's ears, and the press and slide of the warrior's muscles against the spacer's cock pitched him over the edge again as well.

Cradling Samuel close, Arl'ban staggered to the pool's edge and carefully set his lover down. Samuel clutched at him, curling his legs tighter about Arl'ban's waist, not wanting him to pull free of his body. "Please... No..." Samuel begged, and so the warrior tightened his arms, lifted him again and dropped to his knees in the shallower water, where they held each other for long, quiet minutes.

Drained, Samuel laid his cheek against Arl'ban's shoulder and drowsed. Then he felt the world tip, as his lover lifted him from the water. How amazing that he had found a lover stronger than himself. Arl'ban carried him out of the pool, set him on the stone edge and wrapped a towel around him. He quickly dried himself off and donned his clothing. Helping a tired Samuel dress, he led them back upstairs. They didn't speak a word the entire time.

Samuel sat on a sleeping couch as Arl'ban went off into another room. The spacer felt relieved, physically, after the passion in the pool, but he ached for the comfort of Arl'ban's arms, for his solid strength to hold onto. His eyes flew directly to the warrior when Arl'ban re-entered the room in the light robe and pants he wore for sleeping.

Arl'ban stopped to peer at Samuel, who thought for a moment that the warrior looked nervous. Frowning, Samuel waited. "Sahmwell," Arl'ban started awkwardly before he straightened his shoulders, finding his resolve. "Sleep in my bed?" he asked boldly.

Blinking, Samuel stared at him for a long moment before nodding and standing to move to the other sleeping couch where Arl'ban slept. The warrior approached and shook his head, taking Samuel's hand and leading him into another room, where layers of soft blankets covered a broad platform.

Samuel stopped and stared at the bed. He glanced to Arl'ban, eyes narrowing. "Your bed?"

The warrior nodded. The spacer looked significantly out into the main room and to his utter surprise, Arl'ban flushed. Samuel's eyebrow shot up and a smirk pulled at his lips. Arl'ban had pined for him as well? The warrior sighed and walked over to Samuel, wrapping his arms around the man's waist and pulling him close, ducking his head to capture Samuel's lips and still the amused twitching.

"WE'RE going rescue Lan'do?" Samuel asked, leaning back from the table in surprise.

"We can't leave him there," Jack defended. "He's the lifeblood of Sun City."

"We don't know anything about fighting here," Samuel answered in concern.

"You've been training with Arl'ban and the warriors have been planning this," Jack explained. "The gray-skinned natives, they're the Tribe of the Moon. The dark – some of the men here call them Evil's Ash because of the color of their skin. They prey on the light for power. They want to wipe out the Tribe of the Sun."

Narrowing his eyes, Samuel looked over Jack's shoulder at Evas'in. "And this guy is telling you all this. How do we stop them? I'm guessing the light doesn't feed on the dark."

"No. But they'll keep coming after us if we don't do something."

"Sahmwell," Arl'ban said, breaking into the conversation he didn't understand. "You are hurt by the dark." He lightly touched the spacer's healing torso.

Samuel blinked in surprise. "The cat? The black panther? It worked for the dark?"

"It was set on us by the Moon priest. At least, that's what Evas'in said. It was driven by the dark magic."

"Now you believe in magic?" Samuel asked, skeptical.

"Don't you?" Jack asked in a quiet voice.

Samuel turned his eyes on Arl'ban, who watched him solemnly. "Okay. So what are we going to do?"

Looking to Evas'in for a moment, Jack turned back, his shoulders set. "I'm going to find Lan'do while Arl'ban and the warriors fight the Moon warriors. If we can stop enough of them, their power will wane and we'll all be safe." He finally switched to their new language for a few words. "We fight the dark for the sun."

Samuel opened his mouth to protest, but Arl'ban squeezed his hand, and the spacer turned to look at his lover. The protest died as he gazed into hazel eyes. He turned back to Jack. "Are you sure about this?"

Jack nodded. "What else are we going to do? Arl'ban and the warriors are going anyway. Evas'in said the city needs Lan'do, and that if Lan'do is still gone, he must need our help." Again he switched to the language of Lan'do'tay. "He fights the shadows, but is lost."

"The shadows?" Samuel asked, turning to Arl'ban, who looked very serious.

Evas'in stepped closer. "The shadows are dark magic. They eat the light. They eat the life."

Frowning, Jack looked even more worried. "Are these..." he shrugged, "...gods?" he asked, struggling for words.

The older priest shook his head. "No. The shadows are... hungry." He looked frustrated, unable to explain, trying and discarding words as the two newcomers shook their heads.

"I think he means they're predators," Samuel said to Jack in their old language.

"They hunt the sun," Arl'ban said.

Samuel met Arl'ban's eyes, switching languages. "You want this, to help?" he asked awkwardly. "You want me to help?"

The warrior nodded. "With you, I have power," he said softly, and they looked at each other for a long time.

It didn't take long for the warriors to organize. It seemed every able-bodied man and woman gathered weapons and waited in the courtyard. Evas'in conducted a short ceremony as the natives listened avidly. When finished, he called Arl'ban, Samuel and Jack to him.

"For the sun," Evas'in said, hanging around their necks a beaten copper necklace curled and bent into a representation of the sun. They matched the necklace that Lan'do wore. "This is power," he said, tapping the sun that rested over each man's heart. Soon they departed, leaving Evas'in to protect Sun City and those who remained behind.

After four days' treacherous journey, the warriors hid on the last night, determined to attack the Tribe of the Moon at dawn, when their priest's power would falter. Arl'ban sat close by Samuel, watching the spacer as he dozed. Jack noticed, but said nothing. If Arl'ban cared for Samuel, they would protect each other during the battle. They all carried a long knife and a bludgeon. Jack hoped he wouldn't need them.

The sentries warned them in time, two hours before dawn. Huge panthers prowled through the jungle and sprang to attack, and the battle began. Luckily, the sun warriors were familiar with the weapons of the dark, and only a few fell before the monstrous cats. Then Arl'ban gathered the fighters and made for the City of the Moon. There was no sense in waiting now. Samuel ran some steps behind him, the other warriors pounding through the vegetation and passing through the crumbling stone walls that surrounded the dying city of gray stone.

Ash-skinned warriors emerged from the dark to engage them, and the fight exploded fiercely. Samuel tried to stay close to Arl'ban, keeping his back to one of the walls, knowing he didn't have enough skill to fight even one of the pale gray warriors by himself. But he did fight – and he fought dirty when guarding Arl'ban's back.

"There, Jack," Arl'ban yelled over the din. He pointed across the large city. A single ray of golden light shot up into the dawn sky. Several fighters gathered around the spacer to get him there, moving him through the bloody courtyard as the fight for power raged on.

The jungle closed about Jack and the warriors threateningly, nothing like the greenery that teemed with life around Lan'do'tay. Realizing that the loss of Lan'do's power would allow the darkness to encroach upon everything he now loved, Jack became more convinced that the Sun priest must be rescued. For the sake of all of them. A yell of success echoed as dawn broke over the walls – quickly followed by a warning cry, and Jack stopped in his tracks, glancing up in time to see a formless shadow appear in the lightening sky, flying at him, sucking in all the sunlight it touched as it moved. A nightmare embodied, the black hole devoured the air as it flew with a hiss. Jack froze.

"This is power," Evas'in had said.

Closing his eyes, hoping, Jack thought of the blazing sun, and instead saw a vision of Lan'do walking out of the bright light, arms open wide and welcoming, the sunlight shining in his eyes turning them golden. Jack's fear fell away and he felt a great heat erupt from his chest. Blinking his eyes open, he saw the shadow shrinking into nothingness and disappearing with a shriek as a shining stream of pure, golden light obliterated it. Reaching for his neck, Jack hissed and pulled his hand away from the blistering hot amulet.

160 | M A D E L E I N E   U R B A N

"Lan'do, find Lan'do!" Samuel's voice, harsh with exertion, spurred Jack on. He hurried toward the faded stone temple nearly swallowed by the jungle, dark, creeping vines grasping the rock, choking it, digging into it. The enemies picked off the Sun fighters who accompanied him one by one, but the dark continued to wane. Sunlight now poured down upon the temple only to be reflected away by an ever-moving shield of shadows, save one slim, focused beam of light that shot up into the sky through the stone roof of the temple.

Across the city, Arl'ban led the fight against the Moon warriors, who lost numbers and strength quickly as the sun rose. A sharp snapped warning from another warrior got his attention, and he turned to see Samuel holding off a large opponent. Arl'ban took two steps and howled as Samuel collapsed under a strong attack. The warrior rushed the enemy and beat him soundly, tossing the mewling fighter aside and turning immediately to where Samuel sprawled in the dirt.

"Sahmwell?" Arl'ban asked hoarsely as he knelt beside him. One glance around told him his people would quickly dispatch the few dark warriors remaining.

The spacer groaned. "No good."

Arl'ban gasped in relief and pulled Samuel to a sitting position before wrapping his arms around him. "You fight good," he murmured, pressing his cheek to the top of Samuel's head. "You have power."

Samuel smiled, dazed, and curled his hand around Arl'ban's forearm as he leaned against the warrior who rocked him gently. "You are my power," he said quietly.

Jack ran down the hill to the temple steps, stopping short of the swirling shadows. He could see the darkness trying to envelop and cut off the light emanating from the temple. Remembering Arl'ban's words, Jack thought again about the sun and Lan'do while the fight raged on around him. But instead of closing his eyes, he focused on one area of the moving shadows. As Jack stared, he saw a burst of sunlight spread around him, forming its own shield. Walking forward purposefully, he passed through the shadows, like water seeping into solid rock. Hissing shadows snapped at him and closed about him, pummeling the sun shield as he entered the temple.

Completely enveloped in darkness, his protection shrinking, Jack searched for a sign of hope... and nearly faltered, crying out. "Lan'do, help!" He couldn't see anything but the golden light reflected back at him.

"Jahk?" A weak sound, but Jack recognized it.

Jack's heart leapt – the beloved voice dampened by distance but recognizable. "Lan'do? Lan'do! I'm here! I'm here!" he cried out, pushing ahead through the shadows, feeling them give way to his renewed effort. "Where are you?"

"Jahk! Here! I am here!"

Lan'do's voice grew stronger as Jack pushed through the shadows and then the wall blocking him dissipated. His own bubble of sunlight faded away so he could see. He stood inside the dark temple – facing another shadow sphere that swirled around the Sun priest, imprisoning him. Lan'do knelt on the floor inside a shimmering, golden pool of sunlight that barely held the hungry darkness at bay.

Jack's rush forward halted when a man-thing stepped between them, shaking a staff at him and spouting harsh words. Shadows shot out from the end of the staff, and Jack hit the ground to avoid them. The spiraling emissaries of darkness hit the wall behind him and evaporated. The spacer got to his feet to see a nightmarish sight advancing on him: a skinned head, white streaks of paint garish on the burnt, cracking skin, shriveled human parts hanging on a rope about his neck and his waist, even his teeth and eyes darkened to ashes. It looked like a walking corpse. Jack threw himself backward, trying to get away.

He kicked out when the thing got closer, managing to put some room between them. But it simply threw away its staff and jumped toward Jack to grapple with him. The nearly rotting hands closed like claws around Jack's arms and the spacer felt a cold so profound it reminded him of the chill of space. The harbinger of incipient death gave him the burst of strength he needed to throw the priest off, only to watch it advance again with an inhuman howl that cut off short when it threw itself at Jack – and skewered itself on Jack's frantically drawn knife.

The man-thing stiffened in front of Jack, its eyes bulging and mouth spreading into a grim rictus. It stepped back, gasping as it pulled its body free of the tempered metal and looked down at the rent open and gushing gut. The thing covered the hole with its hands as organs started to spew free along with the thick, black blood. With a gurgle it collapsed. The dripping knife still in his hand, Jack watched in horror as the body shifted and bubbled, then melted into a gruesome pile of bone and waste.

"Lan'do?" Jack cried, dropping the knife and rushing to the edge of the shadows.

Shock thrummed through him when he saw the ravages the darkness had worked upon the young man. Exhaustion and pain heavily lined Lan'do's youthful face, and the cursed shadows had cut deeply into his skin. His beautiful eyes – once sparkling and alive – were dull and dimmed. His hands reached out, emphasizing his body that had wasted to skin and bones. But Lan'do struggled to his knees. "Jahk," he called, desperation clear.

"Lan'do, hold on!" Jack answered, closing his eyes and focusing as hard as he could on the vision of Lan'do atop the Sun Temple, arms outstretched. Jack's necklace began to glow as he focused on that image, adding all his energy to it. He closed his eyes and heard Evas'in's chanting, backed up by hundreds of voices – the Tribe of the Sun chorusing to gather and harness the strength of the burning star in the sky above. Without warning, a blast of golden light flashed from Jack's necklace to engulf the shield of shadows that surrounded Lan'do. The darkness shrieked and howled, and when Jack thought he would give out, drained of energy, a small bit of the purest light joined the fight from inside the shadows, and the shield exploded into dark flying shards, throwing Jack several feet back against the stone wall, where he slumped to the ground.

Groaning, Jack tried to sit up, surprised to have to cover his eyes from of the bright light. He cracked open one eye, then both, amazed. The whitest light poured down from the heavens, bathing the entire temple and Lan'do in its power. The young priest glowed incandescent in the sun's glory – his hair and eyes and skin bleached of all color as power bled through him until he was a shining beacon.

The light brightened and flared so much that Jack had to cover his eyes – and then it exploded in a flash that stunned him even through his closed lids. Seeing the white shine as spots in front of his eyes, Jack tried to focus through the now-golden sunshine. When the light had bled away enough, he could make out a refreshed and rejuvenated Lan'do, standing proudly in front of the cleansed altar, arms outstretched to the star above, his amulet and eyes glowing with the power of the sun.

Jack blinked once, and the magical scene was gone, replaced by the very normal young man rushing over to help him sit up.

"Jahk? Are you well?" Lan'do asked.

Groaning at the aching in his back, Jack didn't move, but he stared up at the vision of pure beauty above him. "You are the sun," he said in wonder.

The native smiled as he knelt at Jack's side and folded their hands together. "Thank you, Jahk."

The sunlight's warm rays spread slowly across the walls, renewing the stone and banishing the encroaching jungle, dispersing the last of the shadows, eclipsing all manner of darkness until none existed.

THE whole of Sun City blazed with light to rival the natural sun as the natives celebrated the defeat of the Tribe of the Moon and the triumphant return of their priest. The populace honored Arl'ban, Samuel and Jack for leading the battle and effecting the rescue. Lan'do recognized the large numbers of surviving warriors for their bravery. Food and drink flowed. Laughter and singing rang out. Dancing shook the ground and loving filled the air with tangible joy.

Leaving the celebratory party behind, Lan'do and Jack walked back to the temple, the sounds of clapping and dancing echoing over the stones.

"Arl'ban lacrima Sahmwell," Lan'do said quietly.

Jack glanced over at the younger man beside him. "Lacrima?" he asked, not knowing that word. He'd watched the warrior and his friend sit close together at the party, sharing a plate of food, talking and laughing and gently touching.

Lan'do sighed and shook his head, folding his arms, obviously deep in thought. Jack frowned, but didn't push. It could be many things, he thought. But he'd seen the look in both Samuel and Arl'ban's eyes, and he hoped for both of them that he was right. Samuel would settle better here if he was happy with someone, and his friend certainly lightened the stoic Arl'ban's moods.

They entered their rooms and Jack watched Lan'do walk all the way to the far wall, looking over the pictures. When he finally turned, he looked stricken.

"Lan'do, are you well?" Jack asked worriedly.

The slim man bit his lower lip and nodded slowly. "Arl'ban lacrima Sahmwell," he whispered, and again as he approached Jack, perching next to him on the couch.

Jack tilted his head, heart pounding. Lan'do slept chastely curled up next to him each night, and each night it became harder to keep his hands still. The doe-eyed man was simply beautiful, within and without, and Jack wanted him so much he ached. He'd admitted to himself that he deeply loved this man when they went to rescue him. But Lan'do had made no gesture in that direction.

"Samuel lacrima Arl'ban," Jack said cautiously.

Lan'do blinked and looked up with hopeful eyes. "Yes?" The Sun priest lifted a gentle hand and caressed Jack's cheek, his eyes soft and longing. The spacer realized he'd been missing it the whole time: Lan'do did want him, very much.

"Lan'do lacrima Jack?" Jack whispered his question.

The slim man ducked his head, hand stilling in Jack's hair. For a moment Jack thought he'd gone too far, but then shimmering eyes lifted to his. "Yes," Lan'do whispered. "Lacrisan."

Jack relaxed with a smile, cupping Lan'do's face and pulling his close for a gentle kiss. He moaned when he felt Lan'do's arms close about his neck, pressing his lithe body close. Their kiss turned hungry as Lan'do gasped into Jack's mouth, and soon they pushed and pulled at each other's clothing, desperate to touch skin. Jack felt all his pent-up desire shooting like fireworks within him as this seemingly unattainable gift placed into his hands. "Lacrisan, Lan'do."

Their clothing finally aside, Jack groaned and leaned back onto the couch as a slim hand closed about his hot, thickened flesh, then gasped, shocked as a hot mouth covered him. He couldn't help but thrust into the wet heat, a cry wrenching from him as he felt Lan'do's weight lean against his knees.

The unbelievable pleasure sent sparks flying behind his eyes as Jack writhed on the couch. When Jack's protest translated into a pleasing moan, the other man stopped. Lan'do chuckled and slid up his body, settling their erections together and rutting several times against Jack's hip, his own eyes closing against bursts of pleasure.

Jack moaned, feeling the hot length sliding next to his, flesh catching and rubbing. Lan'do sat up and moved astride Jack, reaching behind him to hold the aroused cock and press it between his cheeks, undulating back against it.

The spacer gasped audibly and cried out "Yes!" as his hips pressed up against the warm flesh.

Sparing a knowing smile, Lan'do shifted again, moving his hips, and before Jack knew it, he was pushing at the tight ring of muscle that led into Lan'do's body. Shocked, he grabbed Lan'do's hips to still him. "Lan'do?" he asked, breathlessly.

The younger man, flushed with desire, looked down at Jack. "I love you, Jahk," he gasped. "Please," he said, his hand moving to hover over his own heart.

His suspicion confirmed, Jack nodded, breathless. "I love you, Lan'do," he said brokenly, groaning aloud. His slim lover climbed off him and disappeared into the side room, but he returned quickly with a small vial. He straddled Jack once more, opened the small bottle, and coated his fingers. Jack panted, amazed at his lover's beauty, and before long his eyes fell shut as the younger man thrust himself down onto his erection, taking him deep.

Their bodies sliding and groans mingling in concert, Lan'do moved on Jack's cock, the bronze suns on their necklaces clinking between their chest, driving them both wild until they gasped and yelled, crying out their pleasure as they climaxed together, Jack buried in Lan'do, his hand stroking Lan'do's erection. And when

Lan'do collapsed to lie atop him, Jack hoped they could always stay this way.

A few hours later, Lan'do massaged his lover's legs. "You learn rest, Jahk," Lan'do said mildly.

The spacer groaned, sore all over from the fighting and the running and the celebrating. "Please. No more talk," he begged. Lan'do had been teasing him for hours.

The priest chuckled and poured more oil into his hands. "No, no more talk, Jahk," he said lowly, sliding his slick hands up Jack's thighs to his hips and then down to his groin, where he stroked with purpose, turned Jack's moans of pain into groans of desire.

"Lan'do," Jack gasped, his eyes wide open as his lover nimbly climbed astride his hips to look down at him impishly.

"Good?" Lan'do teased, sliding his inner thighs against Jack's slicked erection.

The spacer laughed, gripping his lover's hips. "Oh yes, yes, good," he agreed, only to catch his breath as Lan'do reached behind himself, his eyes fluttering shut. Jack could see every reaction as the dark-eyed man prepared himself for his lover.

"I love you, Lan'do," Jack whispered.

"Feel me, Jahk," Lan'do replied, taking hold of his lover's cock and sinking down over it slowly, smiling as Jack's low howl filled the room and echoed off the stone. Unbelievably aroused by Lan'do, Jack could do nothing but thrust up into that grasping, wet heat, burying himself in the bright heaven of his lover's body.

Lan'do rode Jack well, his pleasure clear on his face, his own hand stroking himself until his breath caught and his body seized as he gasped helplessly aloud. Jack would have sworn he saw a flash of sunlight in Lan'do's eyes at that moment, turning them to gold, but then he catapulted into orgasm as the hot drops of his lover's essence splattered across his chest.

DEEP in the night after the celebration, Samuel lay on the sleeping pallet tucked into Arl'ban's embrace, the warmth and solidity of the body behind him giving him more comfort than he would have thought possible. He finally settled, but could not yet rest, so he stirred, shifting to his back so he could look at his lover.

Blinking his eyes open, sleepy, Arl'ban looked much younger than his stoic warrior-self, and Samuel couldn't help but lean forward to kiss him gently, longingly. When he pulled back, Arl'ban's lips curled into a tender smile.

"My lover, my crimin," Arl'ban whispered, his fingers trailing along Samuel's face. "My faryal."

"Crimin? Faryal?" Samuel murmured in the foreign words, lips curving.

Arl'ban nodded seriously, taking Samuel's hand and placing it over his heart, looking at him intently. "My lover, my crimin," he repeated.

Understanding, the spacer pulled the native's hand to his own chest, pressing down on his beating heart. "My lover, my heart," he repeated.

"My faryal," Arl'ban said, very focused on Samuel, who tilted his head in question. The warrior took their combined hands and thumped them in time to the beating of his heart, then moved their hands over his wrist and thumped them in time to his pulse. "Faryal," he said.

"My lover, my heart... My life?" Samuel whispered in his new tongue.

"My life," Arl'ban said, raising their hands to his forehead, then to his lips, then again to his heart.

Emotion swelling in his chest, Samuel felt compelled to echo the native's actions, lifting their folded hands to his forehead, then his lips, then to his heart.

Joy transformed Arl'ban's face, and the spacer didn't think he'd ever seen anything so beautiful. "In sun, in quildasq," the warrior said quietly. "In quildaen, in light."

Some translations later, Samuel lay in Arl'ban's arms, drowsy, wondering about the words spoken. They clearly had deep meaning to his lover, and he felt the strength of them himself. My lover, my heart, my life – in sun, in dark, in shadow, in light. Samuel drifted to sleep, knowing he'd never be alone again.

THE next several days passed quietly, and Jack noticed that Samuel and Arl'ban became inseparable. He smiled every time he saw them squeeze their hands together before parting for short amounts of time, usually when Arl'ban led cautionary scouting trips out of the city. During one such departure Jack came around a corner to hear Arl'ban speaking softly. Then the tall warrior kissed Samuel gently and departed while the spacer watched.

"What was that about?" Jack asked, walking up behind Samuel. The other man's cheeks pinkened.

"Ah, I sort of got married. After the celebration."

Jack's eyebrows rose quickly. "Married? To Arl'ban, right?"

"Of course, to Arl'ban," Samuel snapped before sighing. "Iy lacrimor, iy crimin, iy faryal – my lover, my heart, my life; A lando, a quildasq, a quildaen, a lanche. In sun, in dark, in shadow, in light."

Jack smiled, his eyes dancing. "Ah... Congratulations?"

Samuel smiled and chuckled. "We'll see. I'm probably overplaying it. But he's the one."

Jack squeezed his shoulder in support. "I think he loves you. It's clear in his eyes and the way he watches you. I'm happy for you."

"What about you and Lan'do?" Samuel asked, smirking.

"Lan'do is the one for me," Jack said with a nod. "We love each other. Not sure about the whole married thing, though." Samuel simply laughed.

That night Lan'do offered Jack a small, carved wooden box. Jack looked at it in confusion.

"For you, Jahk," Lan'do said, kneeling at his feet and leaning on his knees.

The blond man blinked and pulled open the box. Inside a carefully hammered ring of copper twinkled from a soft white cloth. Jack's eyes flew to meet his lover's. "Lan'do?"

The priest pulled the ring from the box and slid it onto Jack's middle finger. "I am yours and you are mine," Lan'do said. "I love you, Jahk. You are my lover and my power. Will you stay with me?"

Jack's impassioned kiss told Lan'do his answer.


WATCHING Lan'do bustle around him, Jack sat in the chair, swaddled in a thick blanket, shivering. He wondered how someone could catch the flu in the jungle. What a joke. And Samuel had it even worse the past week with a fever that just wouldn't let up.

They couldn't shake this cold. First they chilled. Then they shook so much they couldn't hold onto a cup of water. Then Jack sweated and groaned and ached overnight, but then he felt better in the morning. Samuel just stayed miserable. At least Jack was getting a couple of days' rest to enjoy between cycles.

Back into the "chills phase" now, Jack felt like absolute shit. Three weeks he'd been going through this cycle every few days. He really wanted to curl up in bed and cuddle with Lan'do, as they had much of the past few weeks since the raid on the City of the Moon.

Lan'do worried about the fever in them both. Illness of any kind didn't settle well with the young priest, who thought he should be able to do something about it, especially when dealing with fever. Jack knew his lover healed others, and many of the natives believed he worked miracles through magic. But despite everything he'd seen in the recent battle and his deep love for Lan'do, Jack had to admit the young priest was stymied.

Each time Lan'do thought he had banished the fever, it came back. In Samuel's case, stronger. Stymied, Jack's lover consulted with Evas'in and a midwife, looking for answers, answers that weren't forthcoming. Evas'in evaluated Jack a couple of weeks ago and shook his head. He thought the fever resembled a childhood malady easily remedied, but they couldn't be sure.

Jack tried to relax, certain he was on the mend although he ached and felt light-headed. Samuel stayed on his mind, and Jack was trying really hard not to fret. His friend's similar illness worsened instead of getting better. Arl'ban had reported that morning that Samuel continued to weaken. He could barely stand and refused all food but broth and water. Jack silently sympathized as he looked at the fruit in front of him and felt nauseous.

Arl'ban ran into the room, surprising them both. He spoke so quickly Jack couldn't follow his words. Even more surprised when the warrior grabbed Lan'do's hand and practically dragged him out of the room, Jack pushed himself up out of the chair, leaving the blanket behind. Afraid Samuel might be hurting, Jack concentrated on standing and moving, although he felt dangerously weak. When he finally made it down the hall to Arl'ban's rooms, he heard the warrior calling Samuel's name in the bedchamber, his voice shaking.

"Sahmwell, Sahmwell, do not leave, do not leave," Arl'ban said in an agitated, choked voice. He held Samuel against him on the bed, and Jack swallowed hard as he saw his friend flushed and staring blankly. He breathed fast and shallow, and sweat ran from his temples to his soaked shirt.

Lan'do stepped back slowly, horror covering his face. Jack watched Samuel slowly focus his eyes, but he could barely speak his lover's name. Arl'ban rocked him slowly and Jack heard the tall native murmur, "I love you" desperately against Samuel's ear.

Exhausted by even the short walk, Jack set his hand on Lan'do's shoulder. The priest looked to Jack, grief in his eyes. "Lan'do?" Jack rasped. "Can you heal Samuel?" His other hand balled into a fist, exhibiting his frustration. The fever obviously was killing his friend, and Jack was at a loss for what to do.

Face tense and eyes filled with tears, Lan'do nodded and suddenly spouted a flow of words so quickly Jack immediately lost the thread of meaning. Arl'ban reacted badly, snapping back at Lan'do, and the men argued at a furious pace until Arl'ban's face crumpled, and he ducked his head, clutching Samuel close.

Shocked, Jack stared. Arl'ban had never acted like this. The spacer stumbled to sit at the foot of the platform. His skin prickled painfully with the cold that threatened to shake him to pieces. Jack swallowed hard and watched the couple nearby. Samuel told him they'd exchanged words of commitment, and that Jack understood. But to see the stoic warrior reduced to such frantic worry...

A wave of weakness struck Jack and he sagged to one elbow. Drained, dizzy, and shivering, he couldn't seem to get his breath. "Lan'do..."

"Jahk, I love you. I am here. Forgive me, please, forgive me," Lan'do said, voice choked with tears.

Not understanding, Jack tried to shake his head, but he couldn't find the strength. "Forgive..." he repeated weakly, and he could hear Lan'do's voice begging him. He could hear Arl'ban's harsh grief fading in his ears as his vision dimmed.

Darkness.

WHEN Jack woke, bright lights, white walls and a quiet beeping assailed his senses. He carefully turned his head, recognizing what looked to be a hospital room. Apparently his waking alerted someone, and a nurse entered.

"Well, Captain Addison, gave us quite a scare, you did," she said.

Jack wrinkled his nose at his much-detested title. "Yeah? Am I okay?" He forced his brain to find the right words. They didn't sound right – sharp and harsh instead of soft and musical.

"Oh yes, right as rain now. Would have been better if the rescue crew had found you earlier, but we pulled you out of it."

"Out of what?" Jack asked, confused. Her words barely made sense. Why didn't he understand?

"Out of the wreck, out of the jungle that was killing you," the nurse said. "Are you having trouble remembering?"

Blinking at her, Jack slowly nodded his head. What did Lan'do do? How were they back here? He didn't want to be held for amnesia, but... "Killing me?"

"You contracted what we call Yageur malaria. It's carried by biting insects and manifests in either cyclical or ongoing fever, chills, aching. Flu-like symptoms, really."

"Yeah," Jack said, sitting up. "But was I dying?"

"You would have, without treatment. The problem with Yageur is multiple bites. Can't get away from the jungle, so you can't get away from the insects," the nurse said wryly. "We administer antimalarials here, but the danger is really in the fever."

"Fever. Samuel had the fever really bad," Jack said, pushing himself up.

"Yes, Mr. Walken. He was much worse off than you. He was in a coma when they brought him in. We gave him the drugs for the malaria and did all we could to reduce the fever. Honestly? He was lucky," the nurse said. "And he's next door, once you feel up to moving around." Jack immediately threw off the blanket and swung his legs down. "Wait a second, let me help," the nurse said, moving under his arm to help him balance.

"I remember my arm hurting... and my leg..." Jack said as they walked slowly.

"Well, we went over every bit of you. Nothing broken, no infection, just a few bruises and bumps and the malaria, of course," the nurse said. Jack frowned harder as he limped into Samuel's room, and the nurse helped him settle into a chair next to the bed. "Go ahead and wake him up, he was asking about you earlier," the nurse said. "I'll come back later."

"They found us at the ship?" Jack asked slowly.

"Yes, we got the report last night. Took them awhile to hone in on the distress signal – some sort of odd interference they never figured out. It blocked the signal for a good week, but then just disappeared. But things like that happen here." The nurse shrugged. "Weird planet," she said, looking at Jack in concern.

The spacer cleared his throat. "Ah, I blacked out toward the end," he explained weakly.

The nurse nodded, turning all mother-hennish. "Well, you and your friend are all fixed up, and you can leave in a few days when you've rested a bit more. We need to make sure the fever doesn't come back."

Jack nodded, waited until she left, then went to find his friend. "Sammy?" he asked, stopping bedside.

The other man twitched and then opened his eyes, a smile pulling at his lips. "Jack?" he said in relief.

"Have you heard what happened?"

Samuel shook his head. Jack recounted the confusing details the nurse gave him. Samuel confirmed Jack's hopes and fears. It all happened. All of it – unless the fever had given them both the same highly detailed delusions. The nurse's words sounded funny because they weren't the right language. The injuries didn't exist because they'd healed weeks ago. They decided to ask for details as soon as possible

Getting them didn't help them feel any better.

"But we were in Lan'do'tay for months," Samuel hissed.

"I know. The nurse said my arm wasn't broken, and there's nothing wrong with my leg, not even a scar. I just don't understand," Jack muttered. Then he startled. "Our necklaces... My ring..." Samuel blanched, grief heavy upon him as he touched his chest.

Once released from the hospital, a search of local history records revealed that an indigenous population once lived on Yageur, separated into several large clans, each devoted to a different deity: the sky and the earth, and the sun and the moon.

The clincher came when Samuel choked over his video viewer, drawing Jack's attention from the history reel he pored over. Jack froze when he looked into the viewer to see the stone pyramid.

"This large temple was obviously inhabited thousands of years ago and it was devoted to worship of the sun," Jack read woodenly. "It is the focal point of the ruins of Lan'do'tay, now on government land and open for hiking and scientific study."

"What the hell?" Samuel whispered, voice broken.

"Lan'do," Jack whispered longingly, staring into the video viewer.

"What happened?" Samuel asked in a thick voice.

"What?" Jack asked.

"What happened to the people in Lan'do'tay?" he asked, gesturing to the viewer.

Jack looked back into the machine, clicking to the next page, which made his heart stop. "Sammy..." he whispered.

Samuel carefully pushed him aside and looked. "Aw hell."

The viewer showed a picture of the drawing from Lan'do's wall: the pyramid with a figure reaching to the sun and a black, smoking streak tearing across the sky.

They drank a lot that night, both utterly torn.

Slowly they uncovered more history, finding out that most scientists believed a meteor must have fallen from space, bringing deadly radiation with it that killed off the Tribe of the Sun and other populations. Few other theories existed because although archaeologists found burial mounds for other tribes, most evidence pointed to a sudden, mass disappearance in the cities devoted to the sun and the moon.

"I miss him," Samuel said abruptly one afternoon as he looked out over the nearby jungle.

Jack looked at him blearily. "Huh?"

"I miss Arl'ban," Samuel said, voice hollow with loss. "At least when we crashed and I left Polly behind, I knew she had Harry and I had you. Arl'ban doesn't have anyone else. One of the last things I remember him saying was that I was the only one he'd ever loved. He was begging me not to leave. With him I felt complete. I loved... *love* him." He choked on the welling emotion. "I didn't want to leave him."

Jack laid his head on his arms on the table. "Lan'do," he whispered. Whenever he closed his eyes he could see his dark-haired lover.

"Look, Jacky, it's doesn't add up. Our time there, the 'interference' that kept the rescue team from finding us, your healed arm, the whole of Sun City disappearing. Lan'do was our priest, right?" Samuel rambled as he wiped at his eyes.

"Yeah. He conducted those services at noon each day," Jack said. "And he was the healer. I watched him quite a bit and the people seemed to think he worked miracles. Hell, I saw him banish the shadows with the power of the sun. I believe he can work miracles."

"Not just a healer, a *great* healer. Your broken arm mended totally in half the normal time or less," Samuel pointed out.

Jack frowned. "So?"

"Lan'do used his power to heal your arm," Samuel said.

"After what I saw when we fought the Tribe of the Moon, I can believe that. What about the rest?"

"He was the representative of the Sun deity. To me, that means lots of power. Maybe a meteor did fall — like we did — and when the radiation threatened his people and he couldn't heal them, he took them somewhere else." Samuel waved his hand.

Blinking, Jack looked at Samuel blankly. "That's a bit much to comprehend."

Samuel kept talking, his mind buzzing with ideas after days poring over Yageur's history. "Say Lan'do froze them in time to mitigate the radiation from the meteor, so it hasn't killed them. So much time passed that they stayed there when they saw the future invading their world. But they can pass through the edges of Lan'do'tay and out into the jungle into modern time, like Arl'ban did when he followed the new 'meteor' to find us."

Jack peered at Samuel, obviously stunned. "And so when we were dying, Lan'do sent us back out to 'now' so we could be rescued," he added slowly, uncertain. Then he blurted, "Why couldn't he heal us? Why send us back?"

Samuel frowned. "I don't know, Jacky. Maybe he didn't know what was wrong. Can't fix something when you don't know how it's broken." He sighed. "Our bodies couldn't handle the illness from their time. Hell. It's not any less unbelievable than us surviving the crash in the first place," Samuel asserted. Jack agreed, nodding as he sat back with unfocused eyes.

"What that means," Samuel said intently, "is that they're still out there. Waiting for us. Don't you see? They've been there 3,000 years. All of them. Those who were killed in the battles did die. We saw several babies born, but I didn't see or hear anything about anyone growing old after reaching maturity. If they were old, like Evas'in, it had to be because they were old when Lan'do took them there."

Staring at his friend, Jack latched on to that idea. "You believe that?" he asked quietly.

"I believe it was real," Samuel whispered, his eyes screwing shut. "I believe Arl'ban is real. Oh Jack, and now he's alone again after being alone for so long." Wrenching pain clogged his voice.

Jack paled, staring at his hurting friend. "I know it was real." He fell silent for long minutes as they sat there. Then he took a deep breath. "We... We could try to go back," he finally rasped.

Samuel's green eyes opened, awash with tears he couldn't cry. The color reminded Jack of the lush jungle and humid heat, of the sun pushing through the canopy and the chatter of birds flying through the branches high above, of the green hanging over and around them, sheltering them, until it gave way to ancient stone, a building lost in antiquity, filled with smiling faces and a lilting language.

Sheer hope fueled their suspicions. A week after they left the hospital, Jack received a call. A nurse had found a cache of their personal possessions in storage.

Jack touched his necklace of beaten copper wire, curled and bent into a sun. He slipped the leather thong over his head, tucking the metal inside his shirt over his heart. Samuel donned his immediately as well, unwilling to be separated from it any longer. But most important to Jack was the copper ring that again circled his finger. He stared at it, the love inside him welling so much he thought he might break down and cry.

"C'mon, Jack!" Samuel called out from several feet away, his pack on his back as he prepared to enter the jungle, eager to go since they'd made their decision. "Which way do we go?"

Looking up into the sky, Jack smiled. "Follow the sun."

They set off walking and the jungle swallowed them and made them its own.

**Madeleine Urban** is a down-home Kentucky girl who's been writing since she could hold a crayon. A longtime science fiction and fantasy fan, she loves to mix those genres with romance to get explosive, satisfying results. She lives with a partner and two canine kids, visits Disney World twice a year, and still believes dreams can come true.

Visit Madeleine's Blog at http://madeleineurban.livejournal.com

## Other Novels from Dreamspinner Press

***A Summer Place*** by Ariel Tachna       248 pages
**Paperback**   $11.99                    **eBook**   $5.99
**ISBN**: 978-0-9795048-4-6               **ISBN**: 978-0-9795048-5-3

Overseer Nicolas Wells had been coming to Mount Desert Island for ten summers to help build cottages for the rich and powerful. Despite his secrets, he had grown comfortable in the peaceful little island town, getting to know its inhabitants and even to consider some of them friends. The eleventh year, however, he arrived to startling news: the island's peace had been shattered by a murder. At the request of the sheriff, Shawn Parnell, Nicolas agreed to hire Philip Hall, the local blacksmith and the probable next victim, in the hope that the secure construction site would be safer than his house in the village. He never expected the decision to lead to danger. Or to love.

***Caught Running*** by Urban & Roux       236 pages
**Paperback**   $11.99                    **eBook**   $5.99
**ISBN**: 978-0-9801018-8-1               **ISBN**: 978-0-9801018-9-8

Ten years after graduation, Jake "the jock" Campbell and Brandon "the nerd" Bartlett are teaching at their old high school and still living in separate worlds. When Brandon is thrown into a coaching job on Jake's baseball team, they find themselves learning more about each other than they'd ever expected. High school is all about image – even for the teachers. Brandon and Jake have to get past their preconceived notions to find the friendship needed to work together. And somewhere along the way, they discover that perceptions can always change for the better.

***Cursed*** by Rhianne Aile       232 pages
**Paperback**   $11.99                    **eBook**   $5.99
**ISBN**: 978-0-9795048-2-2               **ISBN**: 978-0-9795048-3-9

Upon their grandmother's death, Tristan Northland and his twin, Will, come into possession of her Book of Shadows and the knowledge that their family is responsible for a centuries old curse. Determined to right the ancient wrong, Tristan sets off across the ocean to reverse the dark magic that affects the Sterling family to this day.

Benjamin Sterling might not be happy with his life, but it is predictable – at least until Tristan Northland shows up in his office, unannounced and with nowhere to stay. He has plenty of reason to distrust witches and Northlands, but instead of caution, he experiences two unexpected emotions: hope and love

**www.dreamspinnerpress.com**

**Size Matters: Short Stories Long Enough to Satisfy**
*A Dreamspinner Anthology of Gay Erotic Novellas*

| **Paperback** $20.00 | **eBook** $12.00 |
|---|---|
| **ISBN**: 978-0-9795048-0-8 | **ISBN**: 978-0-9795048-1-5 |

### *Snowfall In Seattle by Lucia Logan*

Christopher Booth was just helping out a co-worker, never expecting it to catapult him into the spotlight. When he needs help himself in his new job as the host of a radio sex advice show, he shares some private secrets that lead his longtime friend, Neal Kenelly, to see him in a new light. However, Neal's past makes him leery of approaching the other man openly. Will a more subtle approach be enough to win him Chris's heart?

### *Healing In His Wings by Ariel Tachna*

When the crew of the *Starfire* is struck by a mysterious plague, help comes from an unexpected source: the healers of a nearby planet. First Officer Ryan Nelson is sent to act as liaison officer between the Petari and the *Starfire* and finds unexpected healing in their tender care.

### *Ever Changing by Shay Kincaid*

Born a Changeling, Chase Spencer had fooled his teachers, playmates, even his parents with his altered appearances, but as he reached adulthood, the games took on a whole new meaning. Each weekend it was a different 'persona' and a different partner, and that seemed to suit the young man just fine, until the night he set his sights on someone from his past. Will Chase emerge from his latest game unscathed, or will he be caught in a web of his own devising?

### *Dreamscape International by Connie Bailey & Rhianne Aile*

Visiting dreams to grant paid-for wishes, Dreamwalker Lucien Clarke is the best at navigating the twists and turns of sleeping minds. While recovering from a job gone wrong, he discovers that fantasy's passion just can't match reality's love. Will unseen dangers ruin it all?

### *An Academic Dilemma by Alix Bekins*

Rodrigo is an art history student who finds himself attracted to a new friend while also undeniably drawn to his professor. Exploring his feelings for them both leads him into a strange new world of trust, kink and surprising secrets.

**www.dreamspinnerpress.com**

**Size Still Matters: Short Stories Still Long Enough to Satisfy**
*A Dreamspinner Anthology of Gay Erotic Novellas*

**Paperback**   $20.00          **eBook**   $12.00
**ISBN**: 978-0-9801018-2-9          **ISBN**: 978-0-9801018-3-6

*Sight Unseen by Shay Kincaid*

    Famous actor Jackson Prescott wonders if
anyone will ever look past the glitz and glamour of
his Hollywood persona and love the person behind
the name.  So after accidentally dialing a wrong
number and feeling an instant attraction to Devon
Forrester, the stranger on the other end of the line,
he decides to test the waters … using a different
name.  After getting to know Devon through their
daily phone calls, Jackson starts to worry:  Will the
relationship they've built crumble when they meet
face to face?  Or will Devon be able to forgive
Jackson's deceit?

*Take My Picture by Giselle Ellis*
    Aaron has no idea what he's walking into when he shows up to pose for a
famous photographer.  Instead of being the focus of the camera, he ends up
working as Jake's assistant.  Five frustrating, thrilling and crazy years later, Jake
discovers Aaron has become the focus of his life, a life that's threatened when
Aaron finds someone else, and Jake has to set his beloved muse free.

*Start From the Beginning by Chrissy Munder*
    A heart attack leaves Miles wrangling with a slow recovery and a quiet
retreat … just one cabin down from wounded warrior Drew.  Although he's
unhappy to have his solitude invaded, Drew finds himself fascinated with Miles,
but he can't bring himself to push aside his skittish nerves.  Both men fear
rejection for different reasons, but what if they've instead found the acceptance
they crave?

*Evan's Heaven by Nicki Bennett*
    Actor MacAlester Kerr wanders into a whole new world of pampering and
pleasure when his director sends him to *Evan's Heaven* for a pedicure.  Right
off, he meets *the* Evan and finds himself head over heels.  Mac's on Cloud Nine
when he finds out Evan feels the same.

# Desire Beyond Death: Tales of Eternal Love
*A Dreamspinner Anthology of Gay Erotic Novellas*

**Paperback**   $20.00                **eBook**   $12.00
**ISBN**: 978-0-9801018-4-3           **ISBN**: 978-0-9801018-5-0

### *Ink: The Tale of a Vampire in Melbourne by Isabella Rowan*

After too long alone, Dominic enters a tattoo parlor, desperate to find a way to reconnect to life. He meets Michael, an artist who evokes feelings and needs Dominic knows are dangerous. But those emotions and the allure of the handsome human intoxicate Dominic as much as the blood that keeps him alive, and he finds that he – usually the hunter - just can't resist giving in to his prey.

### *After the Storm by Chrissy Munder*

Angry and frustrated with his chronic illness, Vincent Poulsen moves into an old lighthouse to live out the few days he has left. After a dangerous collapse, he meets the ghostly Captain Cason, who shares stories of his distant past. In the process, Vincent stumbles over the tragedy that binds the captain to the lighthouse and his haunted memories. Then fate offers them both a chance to change the future… for better or for worse.

### *Revenant by Connie Bailey*

When Bo Andressen and his salvage crew contract a job in a crumbling castle, they walk into a mystery of murder, intrigue, hidden treasure and greed that has its roots in the far past. Ghosts are only the first suspected danger – the crew, local constable Gavin Gilroy, castle owner Sir Rhys Turcotte and psychic Tristan Andrews have to find out who of a more earthly nature is involved, before more people fall victim to an ancient spectre who seeks to rejoin and conquer the mortal world.

### *Seeing is Believing by Abigail Roux*

Scott Cunningham has a ghost problem, a problem that requires a specialized touch. Enter Zacharias, Leo, and Andy – professionals, if you will – in solving said problems. But solutions don't always come easy, and if Zacharias and his crew can't get the job done, someone innocent might get hurt.

### *Bittersweet by Madeleine Urban*

His business failing and his marriage floundering, Harrison Holden is falling apart. To make things worse, he wakes one morning to see Piers Claybrook, a man he rescued after a car crash the night before, standing in front of him – the same Piers he'd seen dead in the hospital. Now a ghost, Piers believes he's with Harrison to make a difference in the other man's life, and it's up to the two of them to find the key to living – and dying – and how to walk the line in between without being separated by it.

**www.dreamspinnerpress.com**

Lightning Source UK Ltd.
Milton Keynes UK
14 January 2011

165711UK00008B/105/P